WHAT'S LEFT OF ME

KAREN FOLEY

OLIVERHEBERBOOKS

PROLOGUE

Seventeen year-old Holden Foster hated school dances, but this was the last one he'd ever have an opportunity to attend, the last chance he'd have to finally gather his courage and ask pretty Kate Belshaw to dance with him. And maybe, if things went well, she'd even agree to go to the prom with him in six weeks. She and a group of her friends stood on the opposite side of the gymnasium, alternately laughing and whispering to each other behind the cover of their hands. The theme of the dance was *Vegas, Baby!* and the high school gymnasium had been transformed into a garish casino-themed space with flickering lights, shimmering red metallic fringe across the doorways, hundreds of red, silver, and black balloons, cardboard cutouts of playing cards and dice, and flashing casino signs on the walls, including one that read, *Your Lucky Night!*

God, he hoped so.

He'd had a crush on Kate for as long as he could remember, maybe since grammar school when she'd sat in front of him in Mrs. Cummings' third grade class. Back then she'd worn her dark hair in braids with butterfly barrettes. Tonight she wore it loose, and it fell straight and silky around her shoulders. Wearing a tiered, ruffled dress in periwinkle blue and low-heeled sandals, she'd never looked prettier. Holden was sure of that. He smoothed a hand over his hair and drew in a fortifying breath before taking a step toward her.

"Hey, bro, I've been looking for you." A hand clapped onto his shoulder, stopping him in his tracks. He turned to see Jack Prescott grinning at him. They'd been best friends forever, since the day Jack had come to his defense on the elementary school playground when a group of older boys had been pushing Holden around, calling him *fatboy* and *chubbo*. They'd both fought back until the older boys had finally given up and wandered off to find someone else to torment.

Now, following the direction of Holden's gaze, Jack's grin grew wider. "Ah, the lovely Kate Belshaw."

Holden shook his friend's hand off and scowled at him. He resented Jack's sudden appearance and disliked the speculative gleam in his eyes as he considered Kate from across the dance floor. Good-looking, athletic, and swaggeringly confident, Jack had that elusive something Holden had never had—mad charisma.

"Were you actually thinking of asking her to dance with you?" Jack asked, his voice expressing equal amounts of astonishment and amusement.

"I *am* going to ask her," Holden corrected him darkly.

In just three months, the entire senior class would graduate high school and go their separate ways. He knew for a fact that Kate had been accepted to the University of Maine in Orono, two hours north of Bittersweet Harbor. If he was going to make any impression on her at all, it had to be tonight. They'd known each other since kindergarten, but they'd never moved in the same circle of friends. The only time they'd ever spoken was when they'd been paired to work together on a science project in their freshman year. The other girls had sniggered, but Kate had smiled and moved to sit beside him. She'd been friendly and sweet, never once making him feel bad about himself. She'd been kind. *Accepting.* Holden didn't deceive himself into thinking he was a great catch—he was a big, oversized lunk who became tongue-tied and inarticulate whenever Kate was around. She probably thought he was a loser but if he didn't ask her to dance with him tonight, he knew he'd regret it for the rest of his life.

"Whoa," Jack said, putting a restraining hand on Holden's arm. "Not so fast, Romeo." Leaning in, he took a cautious sniff. "Okay, at least you don't stink of chum."

Holden stared at him in disbelief. He worked weekends and summers with his dad on their lobster boat but he'd never, to his knowledge, reeked of dead fish. He pushed Jack away. "I've got this, thanks."

Jack stepped back, hands raised. "Sorry. It's just that I don't want to see you screw this up. In fact, I'd be happy to smooth the way for you, if you'd like."

Jack and Kate were in several classes together and were friendly enough. Holden eyed him doubtfully. "What do you mean?"

"Let me go over there and talk to her first. You know, feel her out and build you up a bit. She's not going to say no to you if I give you my endorsement."

The last thing Holden wanted was for Jack to step in on his behalf, but his reasoning wasn't wrong—Jack was popular and well-liked. He'd been the starting quarterback on the high school football team for four years straight and held the school record for the most passing yards of all time. The guy was practically a legend in their town. Despite the fact that his grades had been mediocre at best, he'd been offered an athletic scholarship to Texas A&M and would leave soon after graduation to begin football training for the Aggies. As much as Holden envied Jack's easy charm and confidence, there was every chance Kate *would* look more favorably on him if Jack advocated for him.

"Okay," he said grudgingly. "Just tell her I think she's amazing and I'd like to dance with her. I can take it from there."

Jack clapped Holden on the back. "You got it, bro. Wait here."

Holden hung back as Jack wove his way through the couples on the dance floor, already regretting letting his friend intervene on his behalf. Jack approached the group of girls and leaned in to say something, causing them to titter. He gestured toward the spot where Holden stood waiting, and all six girls turned to look across the dance floor at him. Holden shifted his weight and looked away, pretending a nonchalance he was far from feeling. His heart pounded like a jackhammer in his chest and his mouth felt dry. He surreptitiously wiped his damp palms against his jeans. What was Jack saying to them? Why had he let his friend go over there? Why hadn't he just gone himself and asked Kate to dance? Because deep inside, he'd been afraid he would muck it up. Because Kate might look at him with disdain and tell him to get lost. He'd spent too many years being the big kid—the fat kid—to trust his own instincts, even though he *knew* Kate wouldn't reject him. She wasn't like the other girls in their graduating class. She'd always been sweet and kind, which was just one of the many reasons he felt drawn to her.

He glanced back at the group in hopeful anticipation, only to see Jack guiding Kate onto the dance floor. He was leading her toward Holden! No, wait—what the hell? He was dancing with her!

Jack was dancing with Kate.

Stunned, Holden watched as Jack pulled Kate into his arms. He slid one hand around her slender waist while he curled his free hand around hers and tucked it against his chest. He murmured something in her ear and she raised her head to look at him. Holden's heart sank as he recognized Jack's signature smile, the one reserved for when he really wanted to charm a girl. Kate smiled back and inched closer, until her cheek rested against Jack's shoulder as they swayed in time to the music. Over her head, Jack gave Holden a helpless, apologetic look.

Yeah, right. Like he hadn't planned it all.

Holden turned abruptly on his heel and made his way toward the exit, propelled by anger at his friend's betrayal and his own stupidity in having trusted him. He should have known, should have *expected* he would do something like this. He made it all the way to his truck on the far side of the school parking lot before Jack caught up with him.

"Hey, wait up a sec."

Ignoring him, Holden wrenched open the driver's door, but Jack prevented him from climbing into the truck with one hand on his arm.

"Let go," Holden growled. His chest felt tight and achy. He was seconds away from either beating the crap out of Jack, or worse—breaking down in childish, unmanly tears over the unfairness of it all.

"Damn it, Foster, just let me explain!"

Jaw set, Holden spun toward him. "What's to explain? It's my own fault—I should never have let you go over there, should never have trusted you." He gave a bitter laugh. "I obviously didn't learn my lesson when you stole my college entry essay, but I guess that's on me, too. I believed you when you said you only wanted to look at the format."

Holden and Jack had both taken a college prep class where they'd had to write a draft college admissions essay. Holden had been surprised and pleased when the instructor had praised his essay as both strong and compelling and exactly what admission officers were looking for. When Jack had asked to take a look at it, Holden had handed it over without ever suspecting his friend would not only copy it, but use it to help gain admission to Texas A&M.

"What do you care if I used your essay?" Jack said now, but his expression looked uneasy. "You said yourself you're not going to college."

"I never said I wasn't going," Holden said tightly. "Only that I wasn't going right away."

"There's nothing to stop you from still using it. And as far as Kate is concerned, I don't think it would have made any difference if you had asked her yourself." Seeing Holden's expression, Jack put his hands up in a supplicating gesture. "Don't blame me—it's not my fault if she likes me and not you."

In that instant, Holden hated his friend. He wanted to punch Jack right in his smug, handsome face. Jack had everything he didn't—good looks, charm, and an abundance of brash confidence. It was no wonder Kate preferred him. How was Holden supposed to compete with that? The truth was he couldn't. He knew Jack's true character, but who would believe him if he said anything? Nobody. His shoulders sagged.

"Whatever," he muttered. "It doesn't matter."

Jack's expression turned to one of relief. Reaching out, he gave Holden a friendly sock on the arm. "Thanks, bro. I knew you'd understand. I hope you don't mind that I asked her to go to prom with me. I mean, it's not like you two have ever even spoken to each other, right?"

Holden fisted his hands at his side, knowing he'd lost any chance of Kate ever noticing him, never mind getting to know him.

"Just know this," he said, leaning forward so there would be no mistaking the seriousness of his words. "You and I are done. If you do anything to hurt Kate, I'll make you regret it."

ONE

BITTERSWEET HARBOR, FIFTEEN YEARS LATER

The cemetery was quiet at this early hour.

Peaceful.

Situated on a gentle rise of hill that overlooked the Nanick River, Kate couldn't even hear the traffic on coastal Route One, less than half a mile away. Of course, the sun had only just begun to spread its fingers over the horizon, pushing golden beams of light into the deeper indigo of the predawn sky. Birdsong, sporadic and joyful, peppered the silence. Kneeling, Kate placed the flowers she carried at the base of the white marble headstone. Poppies for remembrance. Peonies for love. Purple hyacinth for sorrow and regret.

Daffodils for forgiveness.

And she had forgiven him, though it had taken years. Reaching out, she traced her fingertips across the words etched into the marble.

Jack Everett Prescott
SGT US Army
Iraq
Afghanistan

Feb 19 1989 – April 16, 2018
Bronze Star
Operation Enduring Freedom
Beloved husband, father, and son.

She'd thought she would feel more grief today, on the fifth anniversary of his death, but the passing years had succeeded in smoothing the ragged edges of her pain and loss, like a broken bit of sea glass tumbled by the push and pull of the tide. Now there was just a dull ache brought on by the memory of the day his body had arrived in Bittersweet Harbor and been buried here with full military honors beneath the spreading branches of a flowering dogwood tree. She hoped he was finally at peace.

Sighing, she pushed herself to her feet and turned to leave, only to be halted by the sight of a man standing still and silent near the edge of the cemetery, hands thrust into the front pockets of his jeans as he watched her. Holden Foster, her late husband's friend, had grown up in Bittersweet Harbor and now operated a lobster boat out of a local marina. Kate still had a hard time believing this was the same boy she'd gone to high school with. He'd always been tall, but as a teenager he'd carried considerable extra weight. Maturity and a physically demanding job had melted away any softness and honed his physique to one of lean muscle. Kate was willing to bet there wasn't an ounce of excess fat left on his body.

Just thinking about his anatomy caused a flush of heat to spread through her limbs, followed immediately by a rush of guilt. She had no business thinking about Holden Foster's body, or daydreaming about what his abs might look like, or whether he saw her as anything other than his friend's widow. She didn't know if he came to the cemetery each year for Jack or for herself. She'd never dared ask. Seeing him now caused a familiar tension to coil itself inside her and she suddenly felt as nervous as a teenager. He'd always had this effect on her, for as far back as she could remember. His quiet, solid presence unnerved her and a riot of butterflies took wing in her stomach.

"Holden."

"Hey, Kate." He walked toward her, hands still pushed deep into his front pockets. He wore a faded gray tee shirt and a pair of jeans. Kate thought she could actually see his cobbled abs beneath the soft cotton, and tried not to stare at the way his jeans molded themselves to his long, hard thighs. He stopped a few feet away from her and, as always, Kate was struck by his rugged good looks. Seasoned by the sun and wind, his face was perpetually tanned and there were streaks of caramel in his unruly brown hair. His chin had a dimple in the center and he might have been handsome except that his nose had been broken at some point, and poorly reset. Kate thought the imperfection made him look tough, even a little dangerous. But his coffee-dark eyes were gentle as they considered her. "Are you okay?"

"Yes, thanks." In comparison to his deep voice, her own sounded unnaturally high. Breathless. She paused, gathering her nerve. "You always come."

He lifted one shoulder in a half-shrug. "He was my friend."

She knew he'd deliberately misunderstood her. "I meant you always come when I'm here."

He regarded her quietly. "You shouldn't have to do this alone."

Kate didn't need to tell Holden that she'd been doing it alone since before Jack had been killed in combat on that spring day five years earlier. Jack had loved being a soldier but his frequent deployments had meant she'd been left to raise their infant son, Ryan, by herself.

Shortly after she and Jack had gotten married, he'd

enlisted in the army. They'd lived in a tiny apartment at Fort Bragg in North Carolina. His first deployment had lasted fifteen long months. Kate had been desperately lonely. She'd missed her parents and her sisters. After three months, she'd taken baby Ryan and returned to Bittersweet Harbor. Jack hadn't even tried to persuade her to stay, agreeing that she and the baby would be better off close to family. She'd rented a place just outside the downtown area and aside from family, Holden had been the only one who had regularly checked in on her during Jack's long absences. He'd performed small plumbing and carpentry repairs, ensured her old clunker of a car continued to run, and kept her driveway plowed during the winter months.

Kate didn't fool herself into believing Holden did any of those things out of some special affection for her. She knew it was all part of some unspoken bro-code; an obligation to look out for his best friend's wife. She'd been grateful for his help, even if his actions had sometimes made her feel embarrassed. Holden had seen her at her absolute worst, when she'd had spit-up on her clothes, her house had been a mess and the baby wouldn't calm, and she'd been both physically and emotionally exhausted. Maybe she wouldn't have felt so uncomfortable if he hadn't remained so infuriatingly aloof through it all, seeming determined to maintain both a professional and emotional distance from her.

Only with Ryan had he allowed himself to unwind, holding the baby in the crook of his arm and bouncing him gently as he'd walked around the apartment, giving Kate time to put away groceries or prepare a bottle. Even when Ryan had screamed, his little face scarlet with fury, Holden had remained unfazed. He'd talk softly to the infant, his expression intent, his hands deft and gentle as he'd repositioned the baby against his shoulder. But while his relationship with her son had always been warm and easygoing, the same couldn't be said of his relationship with her.

Even now, despite having known each other for so long, there was an awkwardness to their interactions. He was friendly enough, but in the way that acquaintances were friendly. Sometimes Kate thought maybe he had a personal dislike of her and only helped her out of a sense of obligation. Maybe he blamed her for ruining Jack's life. Why else did he always seem so reticent in her company? She frequently wondered how he would react if he knew she found him attractive, or that her skin felt hot and tight every time he came around. Or that sometimes she had disturbing, sexy dreams about him, where he played a starring role. Jack had been gone for five years but at thirty-two, Kate was still young and healthy. And judging by her body's response to Holden each time he came near, her hormones were in perfect working order.

In the next instant, she mentally berated herself. How could she even think about another guy while literally standing over her husband's grave? She was the worst wife—er, widow—alive.

"Well, I'm glad you're here," she finally said.

"You're up early. I thought I might have missed you."

Kate doubted that very much. Even if today hadn't been significant, she knew for a fact Holden was an early riser. Most mornings, he was out on the water by five a.m. while it was still dark. He liked to say the sea never slept. Her son, Ryan, now fourteen, sometimes went out with Holden on his lobster boat and on those mornings, Holden didn't leave until seven a.m., out of consideration for Ryan's age. Now she indicated her van, parked by the curb. "I'm getting ready to make my morning deliveries, and then I have to be at the diner for the breakfast shift. What about you?"

"I'm working today, so I'll be taking the *Emily Ann* out."

The *Emily Ann* was his thirty-six foot lobster boat, named after his younger sister whom he unabashedly doted on.

"How is Emily?" Kate asked as they walked slowly toward the street. She remembered Holden's sister as a pretty brunette with a bright smile and an outgoing nature. Thirteen years younger than Holden, she was the darling of the Foster family.

"She just finished her freshman year at Boston College, made the dean's list again."

Kate heard the pride in his voice and smiled. "She's always been smart. Is she coming home for the summer?"

"Yes, she has a job waiting tables at the Flybridge Grille, where she worked last summer." He lifted one shoulder. "It's a great job for a college student and the tips are good."

The Flybridge Grille overlooked the busy harbor and was a popular summer restaurant because of its rooftop deck and unobstructed views of the water. "I haven't been there in years," Kate mused, and then bit her tongue in case Holden thought she might be fishing for an invite. Would she say yes if he did ask her to join him for dinner or a cocktail? Her heart rate accelerated just thinking about it.

But Holden made no such offer. Instead, his brows drew together in a frown. "You work too hard, you know that? Between the diner and your baked goods business, it's no wonder you don't get out. When are you going to take a break?"

They had reached the brick sidewalk and came to a stop beneath the boughs of an ancient oak tree. Kate fiddled with the clasp on her purse as she hunted for her car keys. "As it happens, I'm taking a break very soon."

"That's great." His voice was warm with approval. "What are your plans?"

With her keys in her hand, she looked up at Holden. A breeze ruffled the heavy layers of his hair and she could see the laugh lines at the corners of his eyes. She caught fleeting whiffs of his soap, or maybe his aftershave—something woodsy and clean that made her want to inhale him.

"I've enrolled in a four-week culinary master class in New York City. The class is taught by Paul Bellecourt." She waited expectantly for Holden to look suitably impressed, but his expression didn't change. "He has his own cooking show on the Food Channel, and he's published four cookbooks," she explained. "He's earned two James Beard awards and owns the Pâtisserie Amélie in New York City. He's a culinary genius and I'll be learning new baking and pastry techniques from him."

"Wow. Four weeks, huh? What about Ryan?"

"He'll split his time between staying with my mom and my in-laws. I don't think he minds since he knows both grandmothers will spoil him while I'm gone."

"Okay," he said, sounding appreciative. "A four-week class sounds pretty impressive, but it doesn't sound like you're taking a break—that sounds like work."

Kate laughed and gave a small shrug. "What can I say? I love to bake. I really want to open my own bakery, but nobody is going to give a home cook a business loan, not without some culinary credentials. I'm hoping this class will give me some credibility."

"You don't think a bank would lend you money?"

"Why would they? I don't have a degree and I can't even provide proof of a steady work history, since I get paid under the table both at the diner and for my baked goods."

Kate had worked at her family's Elvis-themed restaurant, the All Shook Up Diner, since she was a teenager. Her father was a die-hard Elvis fan and the diner featured his impressive collection of Elvis memorabilia. Business was always good during the summer months, but slowed down during the winter. After she and Jack had married and she'd returned to

Bittersweet Harbor with baby Ryan, she'd begun baking assorted pastry items and desserts and selling them to the local coffee shops and B&Bs. What had started as a way to earn a little extra money had turned into a passion. Lately, she'd begun to dream about opening her own pastry shop, but without a sizeable down payment of her own, she'd found banks were reluctant to give her a business loan.

"When do you leave?" Holden asked.

"The class starts on Monday. I leave here on Sunday."

Holden's eyebrows went up. "That's less than a week away. How are you getting there?"

"I'm driving."

She knew exactly what Holden was thinking as his horrified gaze turned toward her ancient van, parked on the side of the road. He'd been the one who'd kept it running for her these past few years. The van was fine for transporting her baked goods to the various coffee shops and B&Bs in town each morning, but she'd never taken it further than Portland. She only hoped it would make it all the way to New York City.

"No, you can't take that," Holden declared, scrubbing a hand across the back of his neck and looking concerned. "You'll be lucky if it makes it as far as the state line. Even if it did get you there, where would you keep it for four weeks in the city?" He paused. "What about taking the train?"

Kate had considered that, but had discounted it as too costly. The culinary master class itself was shockingly expensive and while she'd been saving her tip money from the diner for months, the cost of the hotel and meals would be expensive. The price of a round trip train ticket would put her over her budget. She could borrow from Ryan's college fund if things became desperate, but she really didn't want to do that.

"It would cost you more to drive," Holden said gently, accurately reading her thoughts. "Between the fuel and the hotel parking, you'll spend more than you would on a train ticket and taxi fare, never mind the risk you run of breaking down."

Kate knew he was right, and yet she hesitated. "I just thought if I had a car I might do some exploring."

"You don't need a car in New York City," Holden said. "In fact, you're better off without one."

"You're probably right," Kate murmured.

"Let me drive you to the Amtrak station in Portland on Sunday," he offered. "I'd feel better if you take the train, otherwise I'll just worry about you stranded somewhere between here and Yonkers."

"Oh, no," she protested. "You don't need to drive me. I have four sisters, don't forget. One of them can do that."

"Let me drive you," Holden insisted. "I don't mind. I'd like to. I have a new pickup truck and she could use a good run on the highway to work out the kinks."

Sunday was their busiest day at the diner and with her away, they'd be shorthanded. If one of her sisters had to take time off in order to drive her to Portland, they'd likely have to close the restaurant early. Besides, she wasn't sure she could pass up an opportunity to spend time in Holden's company. The lure of being alone with him was too much.

"Well, if you're sure..."

"I'm sure." He slanted her a rare smile. "Besides, I'm always hopeful I'll get something sweet in return."

Kate knew he meant her pastries, but for just an instant her imagination surged with all the sweet ways she could show him her appreciation. Her face felt scalded with heat by the vivid, sensual images that flooded her imagination. She quickly turned toward her van, hoping he didn't guess at her scandalous thoughts.

"I'm sure I can think of something," she mumbled lamely. "So I'll see you Sunday? The train leaves at one o'clock."

Holden stood on the sidewalk watching her with that intent, inscrutable way he had. "I'll pick you up at eleven-thirty. And Kate..."

She turned toward him, expectant. "Yes?"

"You'll be okay today?"

Kate didn't pretend to misunderstand. He thought today would be difficult, given that it was the anniversary of Jack's death. But how to tell him she'd come to terms with both his passing and his absence in her life long ago? She couldn't. Holden and Jack had been best friends in high school. There were times when Kate thought Jack's death had hit him even harder than it had her. Whenever she talked about Jack, Holden seemed to retreat into himself, his expression turning closed and tight. He never talked about his friend. So now she just nodded.

"I'll be fine," she assured him. But as she climbed into the van and pulled away from the cemetery, she was aware of Holden standing outside the wrought-iron gates, watching her until she was out of sight.

Holden was at the marina hauling lobster traps down the aluminum gangway to his boat when he heard his name called. Squinting against the sun's glare, he glanced up and saw his sister and another young woman standing at the top of the gangway. Emily waved merrily at him and Holden grinned in return.

"C'mon down," he called.

He continued to make his way along the industrial wharf to where he'd tied his boat up, and set the stack of wire traps down. He barely had time to turn around before his sister launched herself into his arms and hugged him tight around his neck before planting a noisy kiss against his cheek.

"Whoa, you don't want to do that," he advised, laughing. "I'm a mess!"

"I don't care, I missed you," Emily said, stepping back with a wide grin. "Surprised to see me?"

"I am, actually. I didn't think you were coming home until next week."

Emily pulled a face. "We were going to stay in Boston through the weekend, but the dorms are closing tomorrow and almost everyone has already left for the summer, so it didn't sound like much fun to be in the city by ourselves."

"And also, we ran out of money, so..." Her friend extended one hand with a flirtatious smile. "Hi, I'm Samantha Marino, but you can call me Sam. I live across the hall from Emily, but we're going to be roommates next semester."

"Nice to meet you," Holden said, pulling off his work gloves to shake her hand. Sam was a pretty girl, with long blonde hair pulled back in a ponytail, and startling blue eyes. Despite the fact that it was only mid-May, she already sported a golden tan. She wore a cropped white tee shirt that revealed a glittering jewel in her navel, and a pair of slim-fitting jeans that were artfully shredded across the thighs and knees. "How long are you here for, Sam?"

"Oh, didn't Mom tell you?" Emily asked, her brown eyes widening. "She's staying with us for the whole summer. She and I will both be working at the Flybridge. I told her how much she's going to love it here."

Holden hid his surprise at this news, wondering how Emily had managed to sweet-talk their parents into letting her friend stay with them for the entire summer. He loved his sister, but he was happy he had his own place out on Star Island, the eight-mile long barrier island off the coast of Bittersweet Harbor. He enjoyed his no-drama lifestyle, and two college-aged girls would definitely mean drama.

"That's great. Well, I'll catch up with you later, okay? I need to finish loading these traps for tomorrow."

"Oh, we thought you could take us somewhere for an early dinner," Emily said with a cajoling smile. "Maybe the Break-water Pub?"

Holden glanced at his watch, seeing it was nearly five o'clock. Sensing his hesitation, Sam clasped her hands together beneath her chin and smiled charmingly. "Pretty please, Holden? I've heard so much about you, and it would be fun!"

Holden stared at her. Did she actually just bat her eyelashes at him? He gave himself a mental shake. "As tempting as that sounds," he said, dragging his gaze away from Sam to look at Emily, "I already have plans. Sorry, maybe another time."

Emily gave him a pout. "Whatever it is, can't you cancel? I just got home and I haven't seen you in ages! Besides, it's Friday!"

Holden laughed softly. "Sorry, Em. If I'd known you were going to be home today, maybe I could have made other arrangements, but I'm committed. I can't back out."

"So what is it that's so important? And don't tell me you're watching the game at the brew pub."

"No," he replied, his patience starting to wane beneath her persistence. "I need to be in Portland at seven to pick up a friend at the train station, and I still have to go home and shower first."

"What friend?" Emily demanded, eyes narrowed.

"Kate Prescott, if you must know. She's been in New York City for the past month."

"Oh, Jack's wife?" Emily asked.

The question was innocent enough, but it set Holden's teeth on edge. "His *widow*."

"Oh, right. Sorry." She turned to Sam. "Jack Prescott died a few years ago and ever since then, Holden sort of looks out for his *widow*."

"So she's an old lady," Sam concluded. "That's so nice of you!"

Emily laughed, but seeing her brother's expression, instantly sobered. "No, she's the same age as Holden. Jack was his best friend in high school, but he was killed in Afghanistan.

So Holden does things for Jack's *widow* because she's a single mom and life is hard for her."

Holden refrained from telling Emily how far off the mark she was. She was too young to understand and he decided it was none of her business anyway. "All right, let me get back to work. I'll take a rain check on that dinner," he said. "Sam, it was great to meet you."

"Yeah, you, too," she smiled, twirling the end of her ponytail around her finger and giving him an admiring look. "I hope we'll be seeing a lot of each other this summer."

The girls turned away, laughing and falling against each other as they made their way back toward the gangway. "You didn't tell me your brother is *hot*," he heard Sam say before they were out of earshot. Shaking his head in bemusement, Holden finished loading the traps onto his boat. He was under no illusions about his looks and he was past the age where a pretty girl could turn his head, especially one as young as his sister's friend.

The drive home took him through the historic downtown with its pretty storefronts and colorful window boxes, past Harborside Park and the Coast Guard station, until he reached the causeway that led to Star Island. Bordered on one side by the sparkling mouth of the Nanick River, and on the other side by the maze of saltwater estuaries that separated the barrier island from the mainland, the causeway was one of his favorite drives. As he crossed over the drawbridge that led onto the island, he saw the Sundown Saloon, a converted auto repair garage with sunset views across the marshes, was doing a brisk business. His stomach rumbled as he caught whiffs of fried seafood, reminding him that he hadn't eaten since before noon.

He pulled into the driveway alongside his house and quickly climbed out. He'd purchased the cottage twelve years earlier with money he'd saved from his lobstering job. He'd gotten a good deal on the dilapidated house and had never regretted the investment. His father had urged him to buy his own lobster boat instead, but Holden had wanted the house as soon as he'd clapped eyes on it. Ramshackle and in need of a complete over-haul, the cottage commanded westerly views of the marshes and estuaries, but it also had views of the Nanick lighthouse and the mouth of the river. Holden and his father had rebuilt the place over the course of two winters, completely gutting it and replacing everything except the original framing.

The two-bedroom house was modest, but contained every-thing Holden required. Best of all, there was a small barn in the back that he'd restored and converted into a work space where he built outdoor furniture in his spare time. With one large, sliding door and oversized windows, the outbuilding was bright inside and had views of the water. He'd received several offers for the property over the years, good offers that would have seen him recoup his entire investment and then some, but he wasn't ready to sell. Not yet.

He showered quickly and pulled on a pair of jeans and a white, button-down shirt and rolled the sleeves back over his forearms. He ran his fingers through his damp hair to tame it and then, satisfied he no longer looked like a wild man, grabbed his wallet and phone and left the house. Despite the fact that it was a Friday afternoon and the height of the commuter rush hour, the drive to Portland took him less than an hour. He arrived at the train station early and found a parking spot where Kate couldn't fail to see him when she came out. She'd been gone for four weeks and he was anxious to see her. He couldn't remember the last time he'd gone so long without seeing her. In fact, if was being honest with himself, he was tied up in knots, which was ridiculous. He'd been alone with Kate more times than he could count, but after meeting her at the cemetery that day, he'd made a decision.

He was going to court her.

He knew the word sounded old-fashioned and corny, but he couldn't think of another word that came close to describing his intentions. Something had changed that day at the cemetery. He had seen something in her eyes that had given him hope. For the first time since Jack's death, he believed Kate was finally seeing him as someone other than the guy who repaired her car or fixed the broken step on her back door. Unless he was mistaken, she'd finally seen him as a man.

After Jack had died, Holden had given Kate plenty of space, while still keeping an eye on her and Ryan. He wouldn't take advantage of her grief. It had been a heartbreaking year for Kate, since shortly after Jack had been killed, her father had suffered a massive heart attack during the morning breakfast rush at the diner. He'd survived, but a subsequent stroke had rendered him physically incapable of caring for himself, and he'd been moved to a nearby nursing home where he still resided. Holden had worried about Kate that year and had quietly stepped up to do whatever he could to help her, without being intrusive. Whatever his own feelings toward Jack had been, he'd recognized that his death had completely gutted Kate.

Had five years been enough time for her to move on, to maybe take another chance on finding love again? He hoped so, because he didn't want to wait any longer. Maybe she'd reject him, but he had to try. If he didn't, he'd regret it for the rest of his life.

Fifteen minutes later he saw her exit the train station and a wave of something—relief, maybe—washed over him. He had worried about her, alone in the city. She carried a large tote bag over one shoulder, a shopping bag in her free hand, and pulled a wheeled suitcase behind her. She looked great in a pair of wide-legged pants and a jean jacket, with a pair of oversized sunglasses perched on her nose. Anyone who didn't know her could easily be forgiven for thinking she was in her early twenties. She was still slender and still wore her silky, dark hair loose around her shoulders. As she scanned the parked cars, Holden jumped out of the truck and dodged the oncoming cars to reach her.

"Oh, there you are!" she exclaimed when she saw him. "Sorry, I forgot you have a new pickup truck. I was looking for your old one."

"That's okay, I saw you come out." He bent to press a brief kiss against her cheek and his senses were assailed with the scent of her. The subtle, sweet fragrance stirred him, as it always did when he got too close and he had to step swiftly back to prevent himself from greedily inhaling more. His heart worked in hard, swift beats. "Welcome home."

"Thank you, I'm glad to be back." Her face had turned pink. "And thanks again for coming to get me."

"No problem, here let me get that." He took her tote bag and suitcase before steering her across the busy street to his truck. "Did some shopping in the city?"

"Oh, well, not really." She lifted her shopping bag. "I splurged on some new kitchen gadgets. They were being offered to the class at a great discount and I couldn't resist."

Holden handed her into the passenger seat before stowing her gear in the back and climbing behind the wheel. He switched on the engine and only when he had maneuvered the truck away from the busy transportation center did he turn to look at her. She had removed her sunglasses and, as always, her expressive gray eyes undid him. A man could lose himself in those smoky depths. "So, what did you think of the big city?"

"At first, I thought it was exhilarating—the tall buildings, the people, the lights, the sheer energy of it was amazing." She gave him an apologetic smile. "But after a month of the crowds, the traffic, the sirens at all hours of the night, I discovered I'm not really a city girl. I missed Bittersweet Harbor and I couldn't wait to come home."

Holden wasn't surprised. Kate had always been a homebody and seemed happiest when she was surrounded by her family and friends. He suspected she wouldn't enjoy living anywhere except in the small coastal town where they had both been born and raised.

"Did you enjoy the class?"

"Oh, Holden," she enthused, her eyes glowing with recalled pleasure, "it was incredible! I learned so much and Paul was amazing to work with. Really, he's a genius. So gifted in the kitchen, and so *kind*."

"That's great." He flashed her a swift grin. "Feel free to practice your new recipes on me any time you'd like."

Kate laughed. "Well, considering I never would have discovered my love for baking if it hadn't been for you, I suppose that's fair."

Holden gave a bewildered laugh, shifting his attention between her and the road. "What do you mean? I had nothing to do with that."

"Are you serious right now?" she demanded in astonishment. "Holden Foster, it was all you! When I first came back to Bittersweet Harbor, when Ryan was just a baby, you always came by to check on us or to do some little carpentry or plumbing repair for me, remember?"

Holden tightened his grip on the steering wheel. He remembered perfectly. How could he forget? Back then, he'd struggled to confine his visits to just once a week and to keep them short enough that she wouldn't guess he did it for his own selfish pleasure. He'd secretly elated when Kate had moved back to Bittersweet Harbor, bringing five-month old Ryan with her while Jack remained deployed for at least another year. Holden had just turned nineteen and had been young and delusional enough to hope Kate would finally realize it was *him*—Holden Foster—she was meant to be with. He'd wanted her *and* baby Ryan. His secret hope had been that Kate would divorce Jack. He hadn't even considered that his thoughts constituted a betrayal of his childhood friend. Whatever friendship they'd once had, had ended that night on the high school dance floor. In Holden's young mind, Jack didn't deserve Kate.

But Kate hadn't divorced Jack. Instead, she'd remained unfailingly loyal to her husband. Looking back, Holden could forgive himself for believing in his fantasy—he'd been young and foolish and hopelessly in love. Over time, he'd come to terms with the fact that he and Kate were never going to be together, not in the way he wanted. But that hadn't stopped him from watching out for her and her child. His only consolation was that she had never guessed his true feelings.

And then Jack had been killed, leaving Kate alone.

Free. Unattached.

They had reached the highway, but he didn't drive quite as fast heading back to Bittersweet Harbor as he had coming down to Portland. He wanted the ride to last, didn't want to let her go too soon.

"So tell me, how did I inspire you to become a baker?" he asked, slanting Kate an encouraging look.

"Well, whenever you did something nice for me, like plow the driveway or fix whatever was broken—and there were so many things that needed fixing in that apartment—you refused to take any money for your trouble."

"Of course I did," he said gruffly, frowning. "What kind of friend would I be if I took your money?"

"I appreciate that," she assured him, "because we had precious little of it back then. But then I remembered how you always liked sweets in high school, so..."

Holden didn't miss how her gaze strayed surreptitiously over him, likely taking note of the fact he no longer carried any evidence of his voracious sweet tooth. "So you began baking cupcakes and blueberry muffins for me," he finished. "Which was very thoughtful."

"Yes, well, I thought you were the one eating them, but one day Bea Chapman stopped me in the grocery store and asked for the recipe for my carrot cake cupcakes. That's when I found out you'd been giving everything to the guys down at the marina. Bea's husband actually asked her to get the recipe from me!"

"Did you give it to her?"

"Absolutely not!" Kate exclaimed. "I told her the recipe was a family secret, but that I would bake some for her husband. Then she said I should sell them, and that's what gave me the idea to supply the local inns and coffee shops with my baked goods. So I owe it all to you." She turned in her seat to face him, her expression one of curiosity more than indignation. "Why did you give them away? Why didn't you eat them yourself?"

Holden recalled the first offering she'd presented to him—a dozen decadent, oversized blueberry muffins topped with a brown sugar streusel crumble. He'd indulged in just one, because much to his amazement, the long days spent working on his father's lobster boat had begun to melt off the excess weight that had plagued him his entire life. By the time he noticed his clothes were beginning to hang off his big frame, he'd made a conscious decision to avoid the sugary comfort foods he'd enjoyed during his childhood and teen years.

Now he gave Kate a quick, reassuring smile. "It wasn't personal. They were delicious. Trust me when I say I could easily have eaten a dozen of your muffins or cupcakes in one sitting." He gave a careless shrug. "I guess I just didn't want to be the fat kid anymore."

It was the most he'd ever shared with anyone about his own insecurities regarding his weight. And although he strove for a light, casual tone, the confession dredged up all the old feelings of inadequacy and self-consciousness he'd felt in high school. His mother had never seemed concerned about his size, assuring him her three brothers had been built the same way and they'd all dropped the baby fat during college. She'd predicted Holden would have one final growth spurt that would outpace his weight, and she'd been right. The year after graduation, he dropped more than twenty pounds and topped out at six feet, three-and-a-half inches tall. He glanced at Kate and realized she was staring at him with something like mortification in her eyes.

"What?" he demanded.

"Holden. You were *never* the fat kid. Don't even say that!"

"C'mon, Kate, you know it's true. No, don't look at me like that, it was a long time ago and I'm over it."

"I never thought of you as fat," Kate insisted. "You were just...comfortably padded."

Holden gave a bark of surprised laughter. "Oh, so you're saying I had a dad-bod?"

Kate gave him an arch look as she openly appraised him. "I'm saying you looked fine back then, and you look amazing now."

"I wasn't fishing for compliments." Holden had to force himself to keep his attention on the road, because in that brief instant when she'd studied him, he'd seen the female appreciation in her eyes and his heart leapt.

"No," Kate replied, considering him. "That's not your style, is it? You prefer to remain in the background, only stepping forward when someone needs your help and even then you don't want any fuss about it."

After one arrested glance in her direction, Holden kept his

eyes on the road, hoping she didn't see how much her words affected him. She'd pegged him perfectly, making him wonder if it was *him* who hadn't been paying close enough attention all these years. "You know me too well."

But Kate just laughed softly. "I should, all things considered, but I'm not sure that's true. There are times when I think I don't know you at all."

Holden would have responded with a light quip but at that instant his stomach rumbled loud enough to be heard. Kate's eyes widened.

"Sorry," he said. "I lost track of time and didn't want to be late picking you up, so I skipped dinner."

"And I suppose you didn't eat lunch, either. Honestly, Holden, you could stand to eat a few of my cupcakes." She paused. "Ryan is still at my in-law's because I wasn't sure what time I'd be home tonight. Should we stop and have dinner somewhere? I'm starving."

CHAPTER
THREE

Kate knew instinctively Holden wouldn't refuse to have dinner with her if she said she was hungry. He was the kind of guy who would always put the needs of others above his own. Even so, she held her breath until he gave a curt nod.

"Sure. I know a little place in Yarmouth, not too far off the highway. It has a nice view of the water and the food is pretty good, too."

"That sounds perfect. And it's my treat and no arguing, okay?"

"Kate—"

"Holden, let me do this. I owe you so much."

"I don't want your gratitude," he grumbled, but didn't pursue the issue.

The pub-style restaurant he'd chosen overlooked a small harbor. Deciding it was too chilly to sit outside, they found a small table near the windows, away from the noisy bar area. Holden held a seat out for Kate as she sat down, and then surprised her by sitting at a right angle to her so that their elbows nearly touched. As he hunched forward to peruse the menu in his hands, Kate eyed the way his shirt pulled taut across his impressive shoulders. Really, she hadn't exaggerated when she'd said he looked amazing. She hadn't missed how his rugged good looks had caused several women to watch him as he made his way through the restaurant. He held the menu loosely in his big hands, and his strong forearms were covered in a dusting of masculine hair. She noticed his knuckles sported a variety of small cuts and injuries and without thinking she reached out and took his hand in hers, ignoring his start of surprise.

"What happened here?" she asked, tracing a half-healed wound with one finger. "Your hands look as if you put them through a meat grinder."

She fully expected him to pull his hand away, but he curled his warm fingers around hers instead and gave them a gentle squeeze. "Occupational hazard," he said, amusement lacing his voice. "It's nothing."

"Don't you wear gloves?"

"Usually, yes." He turned her hand over in his own and indicated a thin, white scar that traversed the pad of her thumb. "What about you?"

"Well, I don't wear gloves when I'm baking," she said, breathless by the intimacy of him holding her hand. Had he ever deliberately touched her before? She didn't think so, because she definitely would have remembered the surge of hot adrenaline that swamped her, making her feel weak. His hand was so much bigger than her own, browned by the sun and roughened by the work he did. She could actually feel the calluses on his finger as he traced the scar, like the rasp of a cat's tongue against her skin. "I did that on a mandolin."

He glanced at her, his eyes as dark as mahogany. Up close, she could see the lighter striations of amber in his irises, and how thick his lashes were. "A what?"

She swallowed hard. "It's used to slice vegetables."

"Ah," he said, his face clearing. "Now I understand your penchant for baking—no veggies required."

Before Kate could remind him that both carrot cake and zucchini bread required vegetables, a waitress arrived to take their order. Holden released her hand, but as she pushed it down onto her lap she could still feel the stroke of his fingertip across her thumb. After they had ordered food and each had a tall glass of iced tea in front of them, he turned toward her.

"So tell me about your master class, I want to hear everything."

"Really?" Kate asked, casting him a doubtful look. "You want to hear about laminating dough for flaky pastries, or making a perfect mirror glaze, or how to temper chocolate?"

Holden laughed softly, his eyes warm as they held hers. "Okay, not really. I'd much rather sample the finished product, if I'm being honest. But I would like to hear your overall impression. Was the class worth the money you spent?"

"Oh, absolutely," Kate said enthusiastically. "To watch Paul Bellecourt bake was an experience I'd never hoped to have. I wanted to pinch myself to make sure I wasn't dreaming. His skill is so sublime, it was a joy to watch him cook. And he—"

Kate broke off, suddenly conscious of what she'd been about to share.

"He...what?" Holden urged, his eyes gleaming with humor. "Wait, let me guess—he spent the whole time *loafing* around because he had *muffin* else to do. Am I right? I heard he really *takes the cake*."

But Kate was giggling too much to respond except to smack his arm. "Stop!"

But Holden just grinned at her. Kate's laughter died and she stared at him, suddenly transfixed. His smile was disarming. It transformed his face, revealing strong, white teeth and deep indents in either cheek. Something hitched in her chest.

"What?" he asked, turning serious. "Are you okay?"

"Yes. Sorry."

"What were you going to tell me about Paul Bellecourt?"

Suddenly, she didn't want to reveal that Paul Bellecourt, pastry chef extraordinaire and head of a baking empire, had invited her to have lunch with him during the last weekend she'd spent alone in the city. She'd accepted because she had believed he'd extended the same invitation to the other class participants. Instead, she'd found herself alone in an expensive little restaurant with him, enjoying the best lobster risotto she'd ever tasted, accompanied by a glass of rosé and finished with a decadent dessert.

He'd behaved like a perfect gentleman but she'd been uncomfortable, half expecting him to make some kind of pass at her. Instead, he'd put her at ease, telling her she had a natural talent for baking and an exceptional palate for unique flavor profiles. He'd drawn her out, inquiring about her baked goods business and expressing an interest in her culinary future. That Paul Bellecourt should be interested in her was beyond anything she could have ever imagined. He had given her his card when the class was over and told her she hadn't seen the last of him. What that meant, exactly, she didn't know.

What she did know, was that the class had somehow changed her. She no longer felt like a home cook—a hack. Four weeks spent in a professional kitchen, learning and mastering baking techniques under the tutelage of a famous pastry chef had instilled a newfound confidence in her. Now, more than ever, she intended to fulfill her dream of opening her own bakery.

· · ·

"Nothing important," she said now, in reply to his question. "At least, I'm pretty sure it was nothing." She frowned a little in bemusement. "It's just that he seemed to think I have a real talent for baking."

"It doesn't take a genius to know that," Holden scoffed. "You absolutely have a gift."

Kate gave him a grateful smile. "Thank you. He gave me his card and implied we'd see each other again." She sighed, and then gave shrug. "I don't know. Maybe he says that to all his students."

Their meals arrived and it wasn't until the waitress had left that Holden gave her a thoughtful look. "How old is this guy?"

"Paul Bellecourt?" Kate considered for a moment and then blew out a breath. "Oh, late thirties, maybe forty? I'm not sure, really."

"Is he single?"

"I think so." Interpreting his knowing look, she gave an astonished laugh. "Oh, no, no. Definitely, no. I know what you're thinking and trust me, he is not interested in me like that."

Holden grunted softly but didn't say anything more as they ate their meal. Kate couldn't prevent herself from surreptitiously watching him, and felt a swell of feminine pride that he actually thought Paul Bellecourt might be romantically interested in her; that she might be attractive enough or interesting enough to capture his attention. She sometimes thought her own struggles as a widow and single mom might have wiped away all traces of the pretty girl she'd once been.

When they had finished eating, Holden reluctantly allowed her to pay the bill, although Kate could see it didn't sit well with him. She wondered if he was dating anyone and realized with a mild sense of shock that for all Holden knew about her, she knew very little about him, personally. She didn't think he had a girlfriend, but since he rarely offered any information about himself, how would she know? She could easily have asked one of her sisters or even Ryan, who spent a lot of time with Holden either on his boat or helping him at the marina. But if she started asking questions about Holden's love life, people might think she was interested in him. Worse, Holden might hear about it and how humiliating would that be? Especially since he'd never given any indication he might find her attractive.

"So how are you doing?" she asked when they were back in the truck and heading north toward Bittersweet Harbor. "I've done nothing but talk about myself since you picked me up, and I haven't even asked how you are."

Holden gave her a surprised look. "Me?"

"Yes, you." Kate laughed softly. "I meant what I said earlier —even though I've known you forever, sometimes I feel as if I don't know you at all. Not really."

"I'm pretty much a what-you-see-is-what-you-get kind of guy, Kate," he replied. "I'm not that hard to figure out."

"I disagree. I'd say you're more of a still-waters-run-deep kind of guy. I think you don't let too many people in."

He slid her an enigmatic glance. "What would you like to know?"

Everything.

"Do you have a girlfriend?" She adopted a light tone, but her heart rate kicked up a notch at her own daring. She'd never ventured into personal territory with Holden before. It was an invisible line neither of them had ever crossed.

"No."

"Are you dating?"

His mouth quirked upward in the barest hint of a smile. "Not at the moment. Why?"

Kate shrugged and pretended to brush a bit of lint from her

pant leg. "Just curious. You're a good-looking guy, so I just wondered why no one has snatched you up yet."

She felt rather than saw his surprise.

"I'm still waiting for the right girl. What about you?" he countered.

"Me?"

He cast her a swift, meaningful glance. "Look, I know what Jack meant to you. But have you considered getting back out there? It's been five years, Kate. I don't think he would have wanted you to be alone." He spared her one brief glance. "You shouldn't be alone."

Kate's heart clenched hard at the mention of Jack's name and she only just managed to suppress a bitter laugh. How would Holden react if he knew the truth? Jack had not wanted to marry her and once he had, he'd done everything in his power to remain away from her.

She'd been shocked when, during the last few months of high school, he'd suddenly been interested in her. For six weeks, he'd pursued her with an intensity that had been dizzying. Kate had always been shy. She'd never had a boyfriend before and to have Jack Prescott take an interest in her had been both flattering and overwhelming. About five weeks into their relationship, he'd begun to subtly pressure her to have sex with him. She'd just turned eighteen and her embarrassment at still being a virgin, combined with her fear of offending or even losing Jack, had lowered her resistance. He was leaving for Texas in just two weeks and he wanted something to remember her by, he'd told her. He wanted to show her how much he loved her, he'd said.

She'd agreed.

Despite her inexperience, she hadn't been stupid. She'd insisted upon using protection and Jack had agreed. But the last night before he'd left for Texas, they'd driven out to Star Island

and had carried a blanket into the dunes where there were no houses. It was only later, when she was alone, that she realized they had forgotten to use protection. The signs had been obvious almost from the beginning, but Kate had refused to acknowledge the truth until two months after she'd moved into her dorm at the University of Orono—she was pregnant. And Jack was no longer answering her phone calls or returning her text messages. By then, she was three months along.

Her parents, while shocked by her announcement, had steadfastly stood by her, promising to support whatever decision she made. Jack's father had not been so supportive, suggesting Kate had deliberately gotten herself pregnant in order to trap Jack into marriage. He'd even offered to pay for an abortion, but she'd wanted to keep the baby, even if it meant delaying college. Even if Jack no longer wanted to be a part of her life. Heartbroken, she had resigned herself to being a single, teenaged mom when he'd suddenly had an abrupt change of mind and had agreed to get married.

But marrying her and loving her were two different things, as she soon discovered. Shortly after Ryan's birth, Jack had enlisted in the army. Kate had spent most of their married life alone, except for her son. She'd never regretted becoming a mom, but she bitterly regretted not going back to school. There had never seemed to be enough money or time to take night classes and finish her degree. On the rare occasions when Jack had been home, they'd argued about it. Jack had told her she was selfish, but Kate suspected he resented the thought of her earning a degree when he'd been forced to drop out of college. The truth was, they'd both set their dreams aside in order to get married, but their marriage had been anything but dreamy. During the rare times he'd been home, Jack had spent more time hanging out with his high school buddies than he had with her. And then he'd been killed and everyone had called him a hero, as if that should be enough to comfort her. The one thing she could say is that he'd been a decent father to Ryan. He just hadn't come home often enough to make a lasting impact on their lives. Sometimes Kate wondered how much Ryan even remembered of his dad. But she couldn't share any of that with Holden. He wouldn't understand, and she didn't want to say anything that might change the way he felt about his best friend. Let the dead keep their secrets.

"I have Ryan," she said, knowing she sounded defensive. There were days when she doubted she'd ever get married again. She wasn't sure she wanted to give a man the kind of control over her happiness that Jack had had over hers.

"Ryan is fourteen," Holden replied. "In a few years, he'll be off to college."

"So you think I should—what? Start dating? Play the field? Because a woman can't be happy without a man in her life?"

Holden kept his eyes on the road, but she noted the dark flush that crept up his neck. "No," he said in a low voice. "That's not what I'm saying at all. Forget it."

But Kate didn't want to forget it. He'd been the one to open this particular Pandora's box and now that he had, she couldn't seem to close it. "Do you have any idea what it's like living in a small town like Bittersweet Harbor, where people only think of you as Jack Prescott's widow?" she asked, her voice brittle. "The fire department hosts an annual charity raffle in his memory. The high school named the new football field after him! Everywhere I go, people tell me how Ryan is the spitting image of his father and how that must be a blessing to me. I'm pretty sure the whole town thinks I should just stay single and mourn Jack for the rest of my life, as if the memory of him should be enough to sustain me. Well, guess what? I want more. I deserve more!"

She broke off, appalled by her own outburst. She'd said too much, when just moments ago she'd promised herself she wouldn't. Worse, she sounded bitter and ungrateful when the opposite was true. However unhappy their marriage had been, she would never regret Jack because without him she wouldn't have Ryan.

"Kate." Holden's voice was low, soothing her nerves. "Nobody expects you to stay single. I didn't mean to upset you."

"No, it's fine," Kate said, plucking at the hem of her shirt. "You probably think I'm a horrible person. Everyone loved Jack and it's completely normal for the town to want to honor him."

She couldn't tell Holden that she sometimes felt overwhelmed by the burden of being Jack's widow, as if she had no identity outside of that. When the new football field had been completed and dedicated to his memory, she'd been invited to cut the ribbon at the opening ceremony. Every year, when the fire department held its raffle, she and Ryan were there to kick it off and sell the first ticket. The annual prize was a restored muscle car, donated each year by Jack's father, who was a local firefighter, and proceeds went toward a college scholarship in Jack's name. Jack had loved muscle cars and had worked with his father to restore a 1971 Plymouth Barracuda. As far as Kate knew, the car was still sitting in her father-in-law's garage. For her son's sake, she appreciated that the town wouldn't soon forget Jack Prescott, but the public reminders made it difficult for her to move on.

"I could never think you're a horrible person," Holden assured her. "You're a good mother and you were a good wife to Jack. Don't let other people define you, or your future."

"Thanks," she said, giving him a rueful smile. "If I do decide to get back out there, I promise you'll be the first to know."

She felt Holden's sudden attention, but couldn't meet his eyes. How would he react if she invited him to go on a date? Would he say yes, or would he consider that a betrayal of his friend? She found she didn't have the courage to find out.

"I hope so," he finally said, his voice a little gruff. He made a sound as if to clear his throat and then changed the subject. "Emily came home today and she brought a college girlfriend with her. They're both staying with my folks for the summer while they work at the Flybridge. Not that I think my parents will see much of them."

"If they're anything like my sisters were, they'll be out late every night and at the beach on the days they're not working."

As the oldest of five sisters, Kate was familiar with the habits of teenaged girls. Of course, she had taken a very different path than any of her younger siblings, having gotten married and having a baby within a year of her high school graduation. So far, none of her four siblings had married, although her youngest sister, Savannah, would soon tie the knot with Jed Lawson, who had grown up in town and was now assigned to the local Coast Guard station.

They reached the exit for Bittersweet Harbor and turned off the highway. The sun had sunk below the horizon, but the skies to the west still glowed with the remnants of a rosy sunset. The drive took them for several miles along coastal Route One until they reached the harbor bridge that would take them across the Nanick River and into town. As Holden drove over the graceful span of the bridge, Kate sat up taller in her seat and strained to see the water below. Both her childhood home and the family diner were located on Scanty Island, a long spit of land that sat in the wide mouth of the Nanick River and was accessible by a bridge that spanned the Narrows, a fast-moving estuary on the backside of the island.

"I can see lights on in the house," Holden said, accurately reading her intent.

"Probably my mom or Erin," Kate replied. Her mother still lived in the house along with Erin and Savannah, two of her four sisters.

"Did you want to stop there first?" Holden asked. "Let them know you're home?"

"Oh, no! It's getting late and I'll see them tomorrow morning at the diner. Besides which, I'm anxious to see Ryan. I've never been away from him for this long."

"I've seen him a few times since you left, he's doing fine."

The downtown was busy on this Friday night, with the restaurants doing a brisk business and plenty of people strolling the cobblestoned sidewalks. The gaslight streetlamps cast a warm glow over the brick and clapboard storefronts, and the many window boxes spilled over with colorful blooms. Kate rolled down her window and breathed deeply of the clean, salty air. She was happy to be home. She'd lived here her whole life yet she never tired of how pretty and festive the town looked, especially now that the weather was turning warm. She couldn't help comparing the quaint town to New York City, which was colorful in its own way, but also gray and gritty and completely overwhelming. In contrast, Bittersweet Harbor seemed clean and fresh and vibrantly alive. Soon it would be Memorial Day weekend, the official start of the summer season when the local population swelled with tourists. That meant increased business for the diner and for her side business, since the local inns and B&Bs would be fully booked until Labor Day.

"Everything looks so beautiful," she commented. "I forgot how pretty the downtown looks in the summer."

"Sometimes," Holden said, following her gaze, "getting away gives you a new appreciation for things."

Soon they had left the historic downtown behind and Holden maneuvered the big truck through several side streets until finally they pulled up in front of a row of tidy brick townhouses tucked behind a wrought-iron fence.

"Did you leave your lights on?" Holden asked as he killed the engine.

"No. Ryan must have come home early." Peering through the window, Kate saw her unit was ablaze with lights. Even as she reached for her door handle, the front door of the townhouse opened and a boy dashed out, his lanky frame silhouetted by the lights. Climbing out of the truck with her shopping bag in one hand, Kate met him on the sidewalk as he threw his arms around her.

"I didn't know you'd be home," she said, laughing and hugging her son. At fourteen, he was officially taller than her but had yet to fill out.

Ryan pulled away and grinned at her. "I missed you, so I asked Nana to bring me home. I didn't want you coming back to an empty house."

With his mop of sandy hair and his blue eyes, he was a clone of his father, but Kate thought he looked more boyish than Jack had at the same age.

"That was very sweet of you," she said. She peered around Ryan toward the townhouse. "Is Nana still here?"

A woman stepped into the brightly lit doorway and lifted a hand in greeting.

"Ah, there she is," Kate smiled, and then looked around as Holden joined them on the sidewalk holding her suitcase in one hand and her tote bag in the other. "Ryan, take the bags into the house, would you? I'll be right in."

Holden handed the tote bag to Ryan before shaking the boy's hand. "Good to see you, Ryan. Any interest in going out on the boat with me this weekend? I could use the extra hand."

Ryan looked hopefully at Kate, who didn't have the heart to refuse either of them. "I suppose that would be okay," she relented. Once Memorial Day arrived, Ryan would spend his weekends bussing tables at the diner. But until then, she saw no reason why he shouldn't enjoy his free time and she knew how much he loved going out to sea with Holden, even if she worried every time he went.

"Sure! What time?" Ryan asked.

Holden grinned at the boy's enthusiasm. "I think your mother wants to spend time with you tomorrow, so let's plan on Sunday. I'll see you at the marina at seven o'clock."

As Ryan bolted toward the front door with her luggage and then vanished inside with his grandmother, Kate turned to Holden. "That was thoughtful of you. I know you normally head out around five a.m., so waiting until seven is very considerate."

Holden shrugged. "Expecting a teenager to get out of bed that early seems a bit punitive. Besides, I know he'll ask you to give him a lift and there's no reason you need to be up at that hour."

"I'm always up early to drop off my baked goods, but I appreciate that." She paused. "I'll pack you both a cooler, shall I?"

Holden held her gaze, his coffee-dark eyes intent. "I'd like that. Maybe one day you'd like to come out with me."

Kate only barely managed to conceal her surprise. "On the boat?"

Holden shifted his weight and briefly looked down at the sidewalk before lifting his gaze to hers. He smiled and his face creased in the nicest way, revealing the deep indents in either lean cheek. "Wherever you'd like, Kate."

For a moment, Kate was rendered speechless. Was he actually inviting her to go on a date with him, or was that just her own wishful thinking? She'd thought about this moment so many times, but had never believed it might actually happen. That Holden had neatly stepped over that invisible line both alarmed and excited her. Belatedly, she realized he was still waiting for her to say something.

"Yes!" she blurted. "I mean, it doesn't have to be the boat, it could be anything."

Holden laughed softly. "Okay, then. Let me give it some thought. How does next Saturday night sound?"

Swiftly going through her known commitments, Kate couldn't think of anything she had planned for Saturday. "That sounds great."

"Great," he repeated. "Well, I'll let you go catch up with your family and I'll give you a call later in the week."

"Okay." Kate's voice sounded breathless, even to her own ears. Then, realizing Holden had begun to turn away, she reached out and caught his arm. He turned, expectant. "Thank you. For everything. For bringing me to the train station and for coming to pick me up and for being so good to Ryan. I don't know why you do it, but I'm grateful."

Even in the indistinct light, Kate could see his bemusement. "I'm happy to do all those things, and more. Why wouldn't I?"

Of course. It all came back to his friendship with Jack. She was spared a response when Ryan reappeared in the doorway.

"Mom, are you coming in?"

"Yes," she called. "I'll be right there." She turned to Holden. "Well, thanks anyway. I don't know what I'd do without you."

Holden glanced past her to where Ryan still stood in the doorway, waiting. "You always know where to find me if you need anything."

On impulse, Kate raised herself on her toes and pressed a kiss against his lean cheek. She felt him go still and when she pulled away she thought she detected ruddy color along his cheekbones.

"Good night, Holden," she murmured. She turned to make her way toward the house, looking back once to see him still standing at the end of the walkway. "Don't forget to call me."

He smiled, his teeth a flash of white in the indistinct light. "Not a chance."

Kate paused on the front steps of the townhouse and watched as Holden climbed into the truck and raised a hand in farewell as he pulled away from the curb. She couldn't contain her own smile as she went inside and closed the door, then briefly leaned back against it. Holden Foster had asked her to go on a date with him. Suddenly, the future seemed sweeter than her tres leches cupcakes.

CHAPTER
FOUR

Holden steered the *Emily Ann* expertly through the harbor, which seemed to grow more congested every summer. Pleasure boats of all makes and sizes bobbed on their moorings and the marinas that characterized the historic waterfront seemed to extend farther out each year as they tried to accommodate more vessels. As Holden negotiated the busy channel, he could see the waterfront restaurants were already doing a brisk business, despite the fact that it was only three o'clock in the afternoon. Patrons leaned on the railings, drinks in hand, as they watched the boat traffic go past. All in all, it promised to be a great summer.

"Grab the bow line," he called to Ryan.

"Got it!" Ryan stood at the front of the lobster boat, waiting until they were close enough to the commercial wharf before tossing the line and expertly snagging a cleat. He pulled the boat neatly in as Holden cut the engines.

His sternman, John Tucker aka Tuck, who worked full-time on the boat with Holden, secured the stern line before he stepped nimbly onto the wharf and lifted several heavy duty, plastic crates from a nearby stack and passed them over the gunwale to Holden. As Ryan began to wash down the inside of the boat, Holden and Tuck transferred the lobsters they'd hauled in that day to the crates, stacking them on top of each other until each bin was full and could be moved onto the wharf.

"Not a bad day," Tuck commented, when the final bin had been loaded. "Six crates. I'll bring these down to get weighed."

Holden owned eight hundred lobster traps and they'd hauled and emptied four hundred of those that day. He'd also brought a dozen damaged traps back with him, which he would repair and then return to the ocean. After Tuck stacked the lobster-laden crates onto a pallet, he followed the hoist along the wharf to where the catch would be weighed.

"That was a good day, right?" Ryan asked. He was hosing down the deck, clearing away the slime and detritus of a day at sea.

"It was a good day," Holden confirmed. "Six hundred pounds of lobsters and it's still early in the season. Here, give me a hand with these traps."

Ryan turned off the hose and stepped onto the wharf as Holden passed the damaged traps to him. "So are you and my mom dating?"

"*What?*" Holden snapped his head up. "What gave you that idea?"

But the boy only shrugged as he stacked the traps on top of each other, not meeting Holden's eyes. "She said you went to dinner together and I saw her kiss you goodbye."

"Oh, well, that didn't mean anything," Holden protested. "We've been friends a long time."

"But you like her, right?"

Holden set down the trap he'd been lifting and studied the teenager. He definitely was not going to tell the kid he'd had it bad for his mom since he was Ryan's age. "Sure, I like her. What's this about? Why are you asking?"

"I just thought if you did like her, you could maybe ask her to go out with you." He shrugged again. "If you wanted to. I wouldn't mind. She hasn't been on a date in a long time."

"Oh, well." Holden squinted and scrubbed the back of his neck. "I probably should have asked you first, but I did invite her to go out with me on Saturday night. Are you good with that?"

"Yeah," Ryan grinned. "I knew something must be up, because she's been all happy and acting goofy since you brought her home and she's *never* like that."

"Really?" Holden fought to suppress a smile. "Goofy, huh?"

"Yup. Singing and humming, and looking all dreamy." Ryan pulled a face. "It's weird."

Holden laughed. He'd give anything to see that side of Kate. More than that, he wanted to be the one responsible for making her act goofy.

"I just wish she'd stop going on about Paul," Ryan continued.

"Paul?" Holden had to think a moment, even as his heart gave an alarmed lurch.

"Yeah, that guy who taught the cooking class. Since she's been home, it's Paul this and Paul that. She can't stop talking about him."

Holden's buoying hopes took an abrupt deep-dive. Was it possible Kate was crushing on the pastry chef? Was her new dreamy attitude due to Paul and not himself? He didn't know anything about Paul Bellecourt, but had imagined him to be a much older man, certainly no one he should be concerned about. And he *hadn't* been concerned, even after Kate had told him the guy wasn't that old after all. Despite how beautiful and funny and sweet Holden found Kate, she was also unsophisticated and guileless. While he thought it charming, he doubted a celebrity chef from New York City would pursue her. Now he wondered if he might be mistaken and his old insecurities threatened to resurface.

"Well, she's probably just feeling a little starstruck. I guess he's pretty famous in the baking world," Holden said, more to convince himself than Ryan. "I doubt she'll ever see him again."

"Probably," Ryan agreed, looking relieved.

"Hey, Holden!"

Both Holden and Ryan looked around to see Emily and her friend, Sam, standing at the entrance to the commercial wharf. They both wore flowered sundresses and looked too pretty to venture anywhere near the working docks. Holden gave them both a wave even as he noticed Ryan eyeballing Sam.

"Who's that?" the teenager asked, sounding a little starstruck himself.

"That's Emily's college friend and I'm sorry, my man, but she's too old for you," Holden said with a grin.

"Oh, yeah?" Ryan asked, looking askance at Holden. "Well, you're too old for her, *my man*."

But Holden only laughed and clapped the boy on the shoulder. "Yes, I am, and it wouldn't matter anyway because she is definitely not my type."

Before Ryan could respond, the girls made their way along the wharf to where they stood. Holden raised both hands in warning.

"Don't hug me," he advised.

"Ew, don't worry," Emily said, eyeing his rubber overalls with distaste. "We only came down to see if we could park at your house on Tuesday while we go to the beach. It's our day off."

"Sure." Holden was accustomed to letting both family and friends park in his driveway in order to avoid the hefty parking fees imposed at the two public lots on Star Island. "You know where I keep the house key in case you need to use the facilities."

"Thanks. We'll be gone by the time you get back," Emily assured him. She glanced at Ryan, who stood staring with unabashed interest at the two girls. "Hey, Ryan. I almost didn't recognize you. You've grown since I last saw you."

To his credit, the boy didn't actually blush, but he straightened his posture and his chest swelled. "Thanks.

Emily turned to Sam. "This is Ryan Prescott, I used to babysit for him."

Ryan scowled, visibly deflated. "Yeah, years ago when I was just a kid."

"Well, I can see you're not a kid anymore," Sam said, extending a hand toward him. "Not if you're working on a lobster boat. I'm Sam."

This time, Ryan did blush as he shook her hand and mumbled an appropriate response.

"Okay, we need to get going," Emily said. "We only came by to check with you before we decided to just park at your place."

"There was no need," Holden assured her. "You're always welcome."

"You should join us," Sam offered, her smile an invitation.

"Thanks, but I'm not much of a beach guy. Besides, I'm working on Tuesday."

"Well, what time do you get home? We'll be there all day."

"*Sam,*" Emily hissed, giving Holden an apologetic glance. "He's working, okay? And I just finished telling him we'd be gone before he gets home."

Holden watched as Sam pouted. She actually *pouted*, her face a mien of sultry disappointment. "Okay, fine." She cast one last look at them as Emily pulled her away. "We'll be at the Breakwater Pub tonight, if you want to join us!"

"I wish I was older," Ryan grumbled after the girls were gone.

"Trust me, you want to stay far away from that one," Holden advised.

"Why?"

Holden scoffed softly. "She's trouble with a capital 'T.'"

"She seemed to like you," Ryan observed, slanting him a speculative look.

"Humans are funny creatures," Holden said wryly. "They always seem to want what they can't have."

He thought again of Kate. He'd wanted her for so long he sometimes wondered if it was nothing more than muscle memory, or a habit he'd grown accustomed to. But each time he saw her, he knew it was more—so much more. She was beautiful, but the appeal went deeper than her appearance. He admired everything about her; her sweet nature, her work ethic, the love she had for her family, her creativity, her humor, and her courage. Her wide gray eyes were as changeable as the sea, revealing her emotions in a way that would likely horrify her if she realized. Life had dealt her some hard blows and while she'd bent, she hadn't broken.

"Hi, guys."

As if his thoughts had conjured her, Holden looked up to see Kate walking down the wharf toward them. She wore a pair of white shorts that revealed the long, toned length of her thighs. Her faded Red Sox jersey skimmed her curves and did nothing to disguise the pertness of her breasts. He allowed himself a brief moment to devour her with his eyes, before he quickly turned his attention to cleaning the boat so that she wouldn't see his avid interest. If she knew even half the thoughts that ran through his mind, she'd probably run in the opposite direction.

"Hey, Mom," Ryan called. "What are you doing here?"

"I just got off work and I saw your boat as I was driving over the bridge," she explained. "So I thought I'd come by to ask if you need a ride home."

Ryan glanced at Holden, who shrugged. Scrubbing the deck and washing down the equipment was part of the daily routine, but he didn't mind if Ryan wanted to head home and leave those chores to him. Being out on the open sea was one thing, but swabbing decks and preparing the boat for the following day could be tedious, especially for a teenager.

"Thanks, but I need to help clean the boat," Ryan said. "It's part of the job."

"Oh, okay. Well, do you mind if I wait?"

"Not at all," Holden replied. Reaching into the cabin, he pulled a collapsible canvas chair from where it was secured to the interior wall and stepped onto the wharf. He opened the chair for her. "Have a seat, you might as well be comfortable. Do you want a cold drink? *Someone*—" he gave her a pointed look, "was thoughtful enough to pack a cooler with enough food and drinks for three days at sea."

"No, thanks," Kate said. "I don't want to be a nuisance. I'm just going to sit here and enjoy the sunshine. Pretend I'm not even here."

But ignoring Kate Prescott was something Holden found next to impossible. He was acutely aware of her sitting just feet away, watching them as they worked. He couldn't help wondering what she was thinking as her gray eyes followed his progress.

"Was that Emily I saw in the parking lot as I was coming down here?" she asked.

"Yes, with her college friend, Samantha," Holden confirmed.

"She's lovely. And her friend is very pretty, too."

"Holden said Sam is trouble," Ryan offered, his eyes gleaming. "I think she's got the hots for him."

"Oh?" Kate's eyebrows rose.

Holden scowled. "That's ridiculous. Of course she doesn't."

As much as he wanted to end this particular conversation, Kate wouldn't be deterred.

"Why is it ridiculous?" she asked.

He slanted her a meaningful look. "C'mon, Kate. Look at me."

"I am." To his dismay she was, and this time there was no mistaking the feminine appreciation in her eyes as her gaze traveled over him.

Holden's entire body tightened under her leisurely perusal and his blood pumped in hard surges through his veins. "You've been sitting too long in the hot sun," he muttered.

Even now, fifteen years out of high school, he didn't trust that women—Kate in particular—might find him attractive. Even if he no longer identified as the fat kid, he'd just returned from a long day of hauling traps. He was covered in sea salt, sweat, and brine, and the residue of four hundred lobster traps —not exactly the stuff of female dreams.

"Trust me," Kate said, a smile curving her mouth, "women admire a man who's not afraid to get his hands dirty."

Holden gave her a doubtful look, but didn't argue. With Ryan's help, it took him no more than twenty minutes to restore order to the lobster boat. Finally, when everything was to his satisfaction, he hosed down his rubber coveralls before stepping out of them and hanging them on a hook inside the cabin.

"THAT'S IT, and perfect timing, too," he said, as he observed Tuck making his way back from the dockside seafood wholesaler where they routinely sold their daily catch . "How'd we do?"

Tuck grinned as he handed Holden a slip of paper. "Not bad. If you're all set, I'll see you in the morning, boss."

"Yeah, I'll see you tomorrow," Holden replied. Tuck nodded at Kate and made his way toward the parking lot behind the marina.

Holden quickly scanned the numbers on the slip and then pulled out his wallet and withdrew several bills. He handed them to Ryan. "Thanks for your help today."

Ryan accepted the money and pushed it deep into his front pocket. "Thanks. Do you want me to get the bait for tomorrow?"

Holden glanced at Kate, who had stood and was now watching him expectantly. "No, I'll take care of that. Your mom has been on her feet all day and I'm sure she wants to get home."

"Okay, let me just grab my stuff." He disappeared into the cabin of the boat.

"Thanks for taking him out today," Kate said, as Holden took the folding chair and stowed it away. "He loves spending time with you."

"He's a good kid." Holden noted the faint shadows beneath Kate's eyes. "You look as if you're done in. I'd tell you to go home and put your feet up, but you probably have baking to do, am I right?"

"Not tonight," Kate said. "Tomorrow is my day off, so Ryan and I will probably order in and watch a movie." She hesitated, looking adorably uncertain. "Are we still on for Saturday night?"

"I'm counting on it, unless you've changed your mind."

Kate glanced toward the boat, where Ryan was shucking off his protective coveralls. "I haven't."

"I told Ryan we had plans. He seemed okay with the idea of us going out."

"Oh." She seemed both surprised and relieved. "That's

good. I mean, of course he wouldn't mind, we've been friends forever and friends go out, right?"

The last thing Holden wanted was to be relegated to the friend zone, but he'd take what he could get. For now.

"Friends do go out," he confirmed. "I'll pick you up at seven on Saturday, if that works for you."

"I'll be ready," she said.

Ryan stepped out of the cabin carrying the cooler Kate had packed for them that day. Holden took it from him and set it on the wharf. "I'll carry this to your car."

"Ryan can take it," she assured him. "If I know you guys, that cooler weighs a fraction of what it did this morning when I packed it."

"Mom, look inside," Ryan demanded.

With a questioning look at Holden, Kate bent to open the cooler and then gave a gasp of surprised delight. "Lobsters! Oh, Holden, thank you!"

Inside the cooler, nestled on a bed of ice, were four live lobsters. They were some of the larger ones they'd caught that day, ones that Holden had selected himself to give to Kate. "I thought you might enjoy them."

"Oh, we will," she assured him, her eyes shining. "People assume because I live in Maine and work at a restaurant, that I must eat lobster all the time, but I don't. They're still an expensive luxury."

Holden understood. People often made the same assumption about himself, but every lobster he kept or gave away was money out of his own pocket. He occasionally gave some to his parents, but he rarely ate lobster himself. Now, seeing the expression on Kate's face, he decided he wouldn't be so stingy in the future. If the way to her heart was through lobsters, he'd gladly go bankrupt giving her as many as she wanted.

CHAPTER

FIVE

T uesday was a busy day at the All Shook Up Diner. The summer tourists had begun to trickle into Bittersweet Harbor and the breakfast rush had seemed neverending, but Kate didn't mind. She enjoyed working at the family diner and she especially liked seeing her regular customers and getting to know the new ones who had just discovered the iconic restaurant. Situated on a long, narrow island near the mouth of the Nanick River, the diner boasted unparalleled views across the water to the town of Bittersweet Harbor, with its elegant church spires, historic mansions, and abundance of boutique shops and restaurants. From the outside deck, Kate could even see the commercial marina where Holden kept his lobster boat, although she couldn't tell if he'd returned from his day at sea. She had served the last customer at the diner more than two hours earlier, and now she and Erin were closing up for the day.

Erin stepped outside and locked the door. Spying Kate on the deck, she came to help her close the remaining umbrellas over the dozen or so tables.

"What are you up to this afternoon?" Erin asked. "Do you need any help baking?"

"No, thanks. I'm going to stop by the marina on my way home and return Holden's water bottle that he left in my cooler on Sunday, and then I thought I'd pop over to Rowan's house for a quick visit." Rowan was the second youngest of Kate's sisters, and she lived on Star Island. She worked two jobs, which meant she had little time or energy to socialize. "I haven't seen her in a while."

"Oh, nice," Erin said. "Tell her Mom is hoping to have us all over for dinner this weekend, if she's free."

"I'll tell her," Kate promised. "But it can't be Saturday night —I have a date."

Erin stared at her in open astonishment. "*What?* Who with? And why is this the first I'm hearing about it?"

"I can't tell you more because I don't want to jinx it."

"Okay," Erin said, laughing. "I'll tell Mom to plan for Sunday, because I want all the juicy details!"

In the parking lot of the diner, Kate opened the passenger door of her van and removed her apron, balling it up and tossing it on the seat. She pulled her hair free from the ponytail and shook it out, then peered at herself in the passenger side mirror. She looked pale, so she quickly applied a fresh coat of tinted lip balm and pinched some color into her cheeks. Good enough. There wasn't much she could do about her shorts and top unless she went home first to change, and she didn't want to miss Holden if he was, in fact, at the marina.

Climbing into the driver's seat, she eyeballed the oversized Yeti water bottle that lay on the passenger seat, partially hidden beneath her discarded apron. She'd discovered it inside the cooler when she'd unpacked it on Sunday night, and Ryan had confirmed it belonged to Holden. She'd stop by the marina and return it to him. She knew it was the flimsiest of excuses to see him again, but she couldn't seem to help herself. She hadn't been able to stop thinking about him since he'd picked her up at the train station four days earlier. And the other day, she'd felt like an absolute degenerate as she'd watched him hose down his boat. His damp tee shirt had clung to the long, hard muscles of his shoulders and back and had done nothing to disguise the impressive bulge of his biceps. Maybe he was right and she had sat in the sun for too long, because she'd been nearly delirious with longing. She wondered how he would have reacted if he'd known even half of the naughty thoughts that had run through her mind.

She drove across the bridge that spanned the Narrows, a swift-moving estuary on the backside of Scanty Island that separated it from the mainland. The bridge was brand new, a replacement of the old wooden plank bridge that had been swept away during a storm the previous summer. The new bridge was wider and constructed of steel and concrete and Kate acknowledged she felt safer crossing back and forth to the island.

As she turned into the parking lot of the commercial marina where most of the lobstermen kept their boats, she looked for Holden's pickup truck but didn't see it. Climbing out of her car, she made her way to the wharf, gratified when she saw the *Emily Ann* tied up. But as she walked alongside the vessel, it became obvious that nobody was on board.

"Looking for Holden?"

She turned to see Tuck walking toward her. In his arms he carried a large plastic bin filled with bait for the lobster traps. Gulls squawked overhead and the smell of fish was strong.

"Is he here?" she asked.

"No, he had to bug out early. You just missed him." He set the bin down on the wharf. "Is there something I can help you with?"

Kate could easily have handed the drink bottle to Tuck, but instead shook her head, pushing down her disappointment. "No, it was nothing important. Thanks."

Leaving town, she drove along the causeway to Star Island and turned onto the road that overlooked the marshes and estuaries that separated the barrier island from the town of Bittersweet Harbor. She slowed as she approached Rowan's house, noting her sister's car parked in the small drive. Instead of pulling over, Kate continued driving in the direction of the Nanick Lighthouse. Holden's house was almost at the end of the road, with views of both the marshes and the mouth of the river.

Slowing down, she saw his truck pulled up in front of the cottage and a red Toyota Prius in the driveway. She didn't recognize the car, but guessed it belonged to his sister. After an agonizing moment of indecision, she pulled in behind Holden's truck and turned off the engine. She'd never visited him at his house before and felt anxious about how he might react. Checking her reflection in the rearview mirror, she grabbed the water bottle and quickly made her way to the side door of the cottage. Before she could change her mind, she rapped sharply and then waited.

After a long moment, the door was wrenched wide and Kate found herself staring open-mouthed at Holden's very muscular, very *naked* chest. He was shirtless and his skin gleamed with moisture. For the endless second before her brain kicked into gear again, all she could think was that she could shred coconut on his abs, they were so defined. Then she dragged her gaze upward to his face. His expression was a mixture of aggravation and something that looked like panic, and Kate took an involuntary step backward. He looked horrified to see her standing on his doorstep.

"I'm sorry," she finally managed. "Is this a bad time?"

To her astonishment, he threw a swift glance over his shoulder and stepped more fully over the threshold as he pulled the door nearly closed behind him, but not before Kate saw a woman in the shadowy hallway behind him, clad in nothing more than a skimpy bath towel. She didn't have time to make out the woman's face but instinct told her she was not Holden's sister.

"Oh," she said, mortified, suddenly realizing Holden's hair was wet, his feet were bare and his jeans were unbuttoned, as if he'd pulled them hastily on when she'd knocked. She had an immediate and explicit vision of what she had interrupted—him, in the shower with the unknown woman. "You're not alone. I'm so sorry—I didn't think—" Embarrassed and confused, she thrust the water bottle toward him. "You left this in the cooler."

Without giving him time to respond, she turned and nearly sprinted down his porch steps, barely hearing him as he called her name and told her to *wait*. She made it to her van and leaped inside, switching on the engine and pulling away from his house in a spray of sand and gravel. She drove to the end of the road and made the sharp turn onto Atlantic Avenue too fast, her tires squealing. Only when she had crossed the drawbridge that took her off the island did she ease up on the gas, aware her blood was pounding hot and hard in her ears.

Holden was seeing someone. Not just seeing her—having steamy shower sex with her!

Kate groaned in self-loathing as she replayed the scene in her head, recalling how Holden had tried to prevent her from coming inside or seeing the other woman. And he'd been upset—visibly upset—at the interruption, and she couldn't blame him. Had she really believed he might be interested in *her*, a thirty-something single mom?

She wanted to die.

"How could I have been so stupid?" she exclaimed aloud. But what had she expected, showing up at his house unannounced? Only that he might have invited her inside, maybe offered her something to drink, maybe even kissed her. In her lurid imaginings, she became the woman in the shadows, eager to greet Holden as he came home, wearing nothing but a scrap of terrycloth. That's what she got for letting herself daydream —a solid slap in the face.

By the time she reached her townhouse she'd managed to pull herself together, although her insides still trembled with embarrassment. She didn't know how she would ever face him again. She certainly couldn't go out with him on Saturday night, which was a bitter disappointment. She hadn't pegged him as the kind of man who would date multiple women at the same time. Didn't it just figure that when she'd finally decided to put herself out there, the guy she wanted was already taken? The worst part was she'd never guessed.

She sat for a moment in the driveway, feeling ridiculously close to tears. Had she only imagined Holden's interest in her? Realistically, she knew she shouldn't feel so gutted. They weren't in a relationship, had made no promises, and he had every right to do as he wished with whomever he wanted. So why did she feel so betrayed? Worse, she felt like an idiot, having allowed herself to dream again.

Drawing in a deep breath, she squared her shoulders and climbed out of the van. She'd do what she always did when she was stressed or unhappy—she'd bake. But she'd scarcely made it to the front door when the sound of a truck gunning its engine made her pause and glance toward the street. Holden's pickup rounded the corner and he pulled the vehicle to a swift stop in front of her gate, not even bothering to align the truck with the curb. In the next instant, the driver's door was thrown open and he flung the gate wide. He closed the distance between them with long, ground-eating strides, looking so big and intimidating that for just an instant Kate considered dashing inside and locking the door. She held her ground, tipping her chin up as he took the steps two at a time. He'd pulled a tee shirt on, but his hair was still damp. He looked irresistibly sexy and dangerously grim as he loomed over her.

"That wasn't what you think," he said without preamble.

"You don't have to apologize." Unable to hide her own hurt, her tone was aloof. "I shouldn't have shown up like that, without any warning."

If anything, his expression grew even darker. "I'm not apologizing," he growled. "I have nothing to apologize for, except that you were embarrassed."

"Of course not," Kate replied, acutely uncomfortable. "You have every right to do whatever you want in your own home. Your sex life has nothing to do with me."

To her astonishment, he muttered a curse and dragged a hand through his hair, causing the damp layers to stick up. He looked even more aggravated than he had when he'd answered her knock. He made a movement as if he would reach for her and for just an instant she thought he would physically shake her, before he fisted his hands at his side. "Damn it, Kate, I was not having sex with that—that *girl*!"

Kate frowned. She'd never seen Holden look so upset. "Okay," she said, unbending a bit. "Do you want to come inside?"

"I can't. I have an appointment and I'm already late. I just need to tell you what happened so you don't think the worst of me." He drew in a deep breath, his eyes hard. "I went home early to take a shower before my meeting with Mr. MacInnis at the bank and when I came out of the bathroom, there she was —buck naked in my bedroom. She claimed to have no idea I was home. She said she'd only wanted to change out of her wet bathing suit into some dry clothes and would never have done so if she knew I was there."

Kate listened, bemused. "But who was she, Holden?"

His eyes widened fractionally. "I thought you realized—it was Emily's college friend, Sam. The one who's spending the summer with her." He blew out a hard breath. "I didn't even know she was in the house until I came out of the shower, Kate. I thought she and Emily were on the beach. I never touched her, I swear. I just threw a towel at her and grabbed my pants, and then I heard you knocking."

The dismay in his voice was all too real, and Kate could see the truth in his dark eyes. A ridiculous rush of relief washed over her. "I believe you. You were so upset when you answered the door," she said. "If her being there was an honest mistake, I'm sure she was more embarrassed than you were."

Holden gave a snort of disbelief. "Trust me, there was nothing accidental about it. She knew I was taking a shower and she purposely let me walk in on her. She tried to spin a story about how she was just changing her clothes and she didn't realize I was in the shower, but how could she *not* have known? I threw a towel at her and told her to cover herself, and that's when I heard your knock." He paused, reflecting. "I don't think she hears the word *no* very often."

Kate could picture the scene clearly and could well believe Holden had been ambushed by the pretty coed. His agitation when he'd answered the door suddenly made sense.

"Well, she's lucky you're a decent man," she finally said. "If she'd tried that with another guy, she could have found herself getting more than she bargained for."

"She was never getting anywhere with me," Holden said, his tone still dark. "I had to come after you and let you know it wasn't what it looked like. I could never be interested in someone so young or so obvious."

Kate refrained from telling him that he wasn't that old, or that most healthy, single young men would likely not have reacted the same way had they found a beautiful, naked woman in their bedroom.

"What is she, nineteen?"

"Twenty-one, or so Emily said. It doesn't matter, she's not my type."

"Oh, Holden." She had to suppress an urge to laugh, because the scene he'd described might have been any other man's secret fantasy, and yet he was clearly annoyed by what had happened. The knowledge only made her like him more. "What will you do? Will you tell your sister?"

"*No*." He sounded appalled at the thought. "I'll give Sam the benefit of the doubt and agree it was just a mistake—even if I don't one hundred percent believe it. But I can't help thinking she's not a good influence on Emily."

"Maybe not, but I can't imagine Emily would ever do something like that. If you'd given this girl some indication you were interested in her, then maybe I could understand—"

"I never did." His tone was flat and emphatic. "I only met her twice for a total of five minutes. I don't know why she singled me out or thought I would be interested in her."

Kate tipped her head as she looked at him. Was it possible he had no idea how attractive he was, or that his lack of vanity only made him more appealing? She recalled again how sexy he'd looked in his unbuttoned jeans. "How did she react when you tossed the towel at her?"

Holden blew out a breath and looked aggrieved. "She was apologetic and begged me to forget the whole thing ever happened."

"Oh. Can you?"

Kate detected a sudden gleam of wry humor in his eyes.

"Unlikely. That kind of thing doesn't happen to a guy every day, so it tends to stay with you for awhile."

"I don't doubt it," Kate said, smiling in spite of herself. "If you could have seen your face when you opened the door. At first I thought it was me, but then I caught sight of her and I naturally thought—well, you can imagine."

"I'm sorry."

"No, no," Kate protested. "Like you said, you have nothing to apologize for."

"I'm sorry I made you feel unwelcome." He made a soft scoffing sound. "Doesn't it figure, the first time you come to my house and I couldn't even invite you in. You practically ran to your car, not that I blame you."

"Oh, well, you said you have an appointment at the bank, so it's not like you could have invited me in anyway," she reasoned.

Holden gave her a tolerant look and then seemed to recollect himself. "You're right, and I'm late. I told Mr. MacInnes I'd be there at five and it's almost that now. I'm sorry, I have to run."

"Yes, go!" she said, laughing.

Still, he hesitated. "Are we good?"

The uncertainty and concern in his eyes made Kate's heart swell. "Of course we are."

"And we're still on for Saturday, right?"

"If that's what you want," she said, suddenly shy.

To her surprise, Holden took her by the shoulders and tipped his head down to look into her eyes. His voice was gruff. "Of course it's what I want, Kate."

Before she could guess his intent, he covered her mouth with his. For just a second, she was too startled to respond. When she didn't immediately pull away, he exerted gentle pressure and Kate's lips parted beneath the lush invitation. Holden deepened the kiss, and Kate unwittingly slid a hand to one hard shoulder, straining for more of the sweet, hot contact. She wasn't sure how long the kiss went on, but when he finally broke away, his breathing was uneven. A little dazed, Kate stepped back.

"I'm sorry, but I really need to go. I'm already late." His eyes, as dark as bittersweet chocolate, smiled down at her. "I'll pick you up at seven on Saturday."

Then he was jogging back toward his truck before she had a chance to respond. He pulled away from the curb, lifting his hand in a brief farewell. Breathless and dazed, Kate leaned against the porch railing and watched the truck until it turned the corner at the end of the street. Even then, she stood for a moment, her fingers tracing her lips where his had been. Then, smiling, she turned and went into the house on legs that had gone a little wobbly.

CHAPTER
SIX

Surveying himself critically in the mirror, Holden swept a hand through his hair in an attempt to tame the unruly waves. He wasn't vain, but he wanted to look good. He was picking Kate up in just fifteen minutes. Their first bona fide date. He shouldn't feel this nervous. He'd known her forever.

Hell, he'd *kissed* her.

He hadn't planned that, but seeing the uncertainty in her eyes when she'd asked if they were still on for their date, he'd known of just one way to reassure her that he wanted to see her. That he wanted her.

God, did he want her. For more years than he cared to admit. He didn't think there was anything she could say or do to change that.

He'd seen her at her worst, when she'd been lonely and exhausted and at her wits' end when Ryan had been a baby. He'd watched her heart slowly break into bits each time Jack had deployed, and had seen the bleak emptiness in her eyes when his body had been shipped home to its final resting place in the local cemetery. But he'd also seen the joy on her face when she was with her son, or her sisters and parents, and she was always genuinely delighted when she ran into friends in town. Despite everything she had been through, she remained sweetly optimistic. He'd spent countless hours in her apartment doing odd jobs and he'd become familiar with her habits. She hummed when she baked and she guffawed at the dumbest jokes. She was smart, too. She'd graduated near the top of their class in high school. She could have finished college and done anything she wanted, but had chosen to stay in Bittersweet Harbor and raise her child, instead. Most importantly, she was kind. Genuinely, deep in her bones kind. Holden liked being around her and he liked who he was when he was with her. She made him want to be a better man.

When Kate and Jack had gotten married, Holden had believed she was lost to him forever. He'd had relationships, of course. He wasn't a monk, even if it had taken several years for him to gather enough self-confidence to approach a woman. Holden didn't fool himself into believing he deserved Kate, but he'd waited a long time for this night. He didn't want to screw it up.

She answered the door before the chime of the doorbell faded, looking effortlessly pretty in a sleeveless black dress that skimmed her curves and emphasized her slim, toned arms. She carried a light sweater over her arm and a small purse. She smiled when she saw Holden, but he saw an awareness in her gray eyes that hadn't been there before.

"You look nice." Her gaze traveled over him in a way that made Holden want to suck in his stomach and square his shoulders for best effect.

"You look gorgeous," he said instead, holding out an arm. "But then, you always do."

He didn't miss the color that rose in her cheeks as she closed the door behind her and then took his arm. "Thank you," she murmured, and a choked laugh escaped her.

"What? Why are you laughing?" Holden couldn't prevent his own grin as he opened the gate at the end of the walkway and let her precede him through. He loved hearing her laugh.

"It's just so strange to hear you say that when literally, for the past fifteen years, you've hardly noticed me," she replied.

Holden was so surprised he couldn't formulate a response. Had she really thought he hadn't noticed her? She'd been the single, white-hot center of his universe for as long as he could remember and she thought he hadn't *noticed* her? He opened the passenger door to his pickup truck and handed her in and only when she was seated and on eye level with him did he reply. Bracing one hand on the doorframe above her head and the other hand on the door itself, he leaned in so that he was looking directly into her eyes.

"I did notice you, Kate," he said, all traces of humor gone. "I noticed everything."

Her only response was a slight widening of her gray eyes. Holden stepped back and closed her door, his heart thumping hard in his chest. That was as close as he'd ever come to telling her how he felt about her. He should have said something years ago, but she had never seemed receptive before. When he climbed into the driver's seat, she looked anxiously at him.

"I didn't mean you never notice me," she blurted. "I know that you've always been there for me and Ryan and that you went out of your way to make sure we were okay during—when we were alone." She mangled the strap of her purse in her fingers. "I just meant you never seemed to notice whether I looked good, bad, or whatever." She was beet red with embarrassment. "You know what? I'm just going to stop talking."

Holden turned in his seat to face her. "If I've never told you how great you look, it's because I didn't want to make you uncomfortable. But trust me, I always noticed."

"Thank you." She flashed him a swift smile. "Where are we going, by the way?"

Holden switched on the engine and eased the big truck away from the curb. "Have you been to Luigi's yet?"

"That's the new Italian restaurant over on Pearl Street, right? I haven't eaten there yet, but I've heard really great things about the food."

Tucked onto a tree-lined street away from the downtown, the restaurant was located in an older, Italianate mansion with tall, narrow windows and an ornate, square cupola above the overhanging roof.

"Oh, how pretty!" Kate exclaimed as they drew up in front of the restaurant. Through the paned windows of a large, enclosed sunroom, they could see the tables were filling up. Soft light spilled onto the walkway as they made their way toward the front door and Kate lifted her nose to sniff appreciatively. "Something smells amazing."

They were greeted inside by a pretty hostess who took Holden's name and indicated they should follow her. Holden placed a light hand at the small of Kate's back as they made their way through several dining rooms. Each room was decorated in a classic Italianate style and provided an intimate atmosphere for the diners. Soft music, urns of flowers, and indirect lighting completed the romantic vibe. Holden had a moment of panic, wondering if he might not have overdone it. This was a spot for lovers. But as he held Kate's chair for her, she gave him a smile that made his heart skip.

"This place is beautiful, Holden."

"I'm glad you approve." He sat facing her, watching her expression as a waiter poured water and told them about the dinner specials. She listened, rapt, and cast Holden a meaningful look when one of the specials was lobster fra diavolo.

"I don't think we'll be ordering *that*," she said, after the waiter had left.

"Yeah, I can't see myself eating lobster tonight," he agreed. "What would you like to drink? I could order a bottle of wine, if you'd like."

"Whatever you want. I'll leave it to you."

"Tell me what you want to eat and then I'll choose."

She perused the menu, a small frown puckering the smoothness of her brow. "Hmm, it's so hard to decide. What are you getting?"

"Definitely the puttanesca."

"I think I'll have the creamy Tuscan shrimp."

The waiter returned with a small basket of pillowy rosemary and garlic focaccia bread, and Holden ordered a bottle of wine and eggplant rollatini to share, before giving him their food orders.

After the waiter had left, Kate looked around them with interest. A large fireplace with an ornate mantel dominated the room, and wide, arched doorways flanked by white pillars led into the other dining areas. The restaurant was nearly full and Holden saw Kate's eyes widen. Following her gaze, he saw an older couple seated in the next dining room, and nearly groaned aloud.

"What are the chances they would be here tonight?" Kate whispered, dragging her gaze away from her former mother and father-in-law. "If they see us, they will definitely get the wrong idea."

Holden refrained from telling her they would have exactly the right idea when they saw him with Kate. He'd known Brian and Helen Prescott for nearly his entire life, had spent many days at their house when he and Jack had been kids. Brian was a classic car addict and he'd always had one or two clunkers in his garage in various stages of restoration. Both Holden and Jack had spent endless hours helping Brian put those vehicles together, but the memories weren't all great. Brian had been a harsh mentor with a short temper, and more than once he'd cuffed Jack for handing him the wrong tool or installing a part incorrectly. Holden knew how much Jack had itched to escape his childhood home and Texas A&M had seemed almost too perfect to be true.

In fact, it had been.

Holden hadn't seen either Brian or Helen in about four months. He pushed down the guilt that stabbed at him, because he *had* been avoiding them. He didn't know how they might react when they learned he was interested in Kate.

Reaching across the table, he covered Kate's hand. "They can't begrudge you a dinner date. Jack's been gone for five years."

He wasn't sure if his words were meant to reassure her or himself.

Her fingers clung to his and he could see the worry and hope in her eyes. "But you were his best friend. What will they think?"

"It's just dinner, Kate. Let them think what they want," he said, his voice betraying his growing impatience with the subject. "You're a grown woman. You're entitled to do what you like, to date whomever you want."

"I know, but sometimes I feel so guilty."

Holden frowned. "Why? What do you have to feel guilty about?"

She carefully pulled her hand free and pushed it onto her lap, lowering her gaze. "Sometimes I think if Jack hadn't married me, if he had stayed in Texas and just paid child support for Ryan, he would still be alive. Maybe he'd even be playing for the NFL." She slid a covert look in the direction of her former father-in-law. "Sometimes I get the feeling Brian blames me."

For a moment, Holden couldn't speak. He hoped his face didn't betray his own guilt at the role he'd played in persuading Jack—however forcibly—to marry Kate. How would she react if she knew? He hoped he never found out.

He recalled again that long, hot summer following their high school graduation. Jack and Kate had been a couple, but Jack had been all about the upcoming football season at Texas A&M. He'd talked about it endlessly, how he couldn't wait to get the hell out of Dodge and start his new life. Fall training camp began the first day of August, and Jack would leave Bittersweet Harbor the last week in July, a full five weeks before Kate would leave for college. Holden didn't need to be a math whiz to know that's when Ryan had been conceived, right before Jack had left town. Maybe Jack had been too buzzed about his future to take precautions, but that didn't excuse his behavior later, when he'd learned about the baby. Holden couldn't think about that summer without feeling his own share of guilt, because he'd wanted Jack gone. He'd harbored a secret hope that maybe, with time and distance, Kate would forget about Jack. But that was before she had discovered she was pregnant.

"Listen," he said now, leaning across the table toward Kate. "You have nothing to feel guilty about. You didn't force Jack to do anything. He could have stayed in college, but he chose not to. He also had plenty of opportunities here in Bittersweet Harbor but he was dead set on joining the army. He knew the risks when he decided to enlist. He made his choice and that's not on you. There's no point in speculating about what might have been, okay? You'll only make yourself crazy."

She was prevented from replying when the waiter returned with a bottle of wine and their baked rollatini. After the waiter left, Kate took a sip of her wine and considered Holden over the rim of her glass.

"Do you blame me?"

"*What?*" Holden made a soft scoffing sound and served them each a portion of the baked eggplant. "Of course not. Why would I?"

"But he was your best friend."

"You keep saying that, but it doesn't mean I was blind to his faults, Kate."

"Do you remember that day you drove up to Orono to see me?"

There were times when Holden wished he could forget. Kate had been at college for just over two months when he'd run into her mother, Pauline, at a local department store, looking at a display of dorm-sized refrigerators. When he'd learned the appliance was for Kate, he'd offered to drive it up to Orono and deliver it to her. Pauline had been grateful. With an iconic diner to run, as well as four younger daughters ranging in ages from nine to sixteen, she and her husband had had enough to contend with. Holden had been more than happy to make the two-hour trip north, since it would allow him to see Kate. He hadn't cared how transparent or flimsy the excuse. But the instant he saw Kate's face, he'd known something was terribly wrong.

"I remember," he said simply.

"I'm pretty sure all I did was bawl on your shoulder." She gave him a wan smile. "No wonder you didn't stay very long. You seemed upset, so I thought maybe you blamed me or thought I'd ruined Jack's future by getting myself pregnant."

"Kate..." Holden couldn't keep the dismay out of his voice any more than he could prevent himself from reaching across the table for her hand. "I never blamed you and I never thought you'd ruined his future." If anything, the opposite was true. The memory of how unhappy Kate had been made his voice rougher than usual. "He was lucky to have you."

"So you weren't upset when you left that day?"

He hadn't been upset; he'd been furious. Kate had been pregnant and scared and Jack had stopped returning her calls. He'd wanted to seriously hurt the bastard. More than anything, Holden had wanted to be her hero that day. If he'd thought for an instant she would have him, he would have married her and raised Ryan as his own. But if he wasn't blind to Jack's faults, he definitely hadn't been blind to his own. At eighteen, he'd been overweight and self-conscious. He'd still lived at home and worked on his father's lobster boat. He'd been nobody's hero, so he'd done the only thing he could do—he'd caught a flight to Texas and had confronted Jack.

"If I was upset," he said carefully, "it was only because you were so unhappy. I'm just glad Jack came to his senses and realized how much he loved you."

It was a bald-faced lie, but he could never tell Kate about that day on the campus of Texas A&M. He only hoped she never found out.

"Oh, right," Kate said, a rueful smile tugging her mouth. "He loved me so much that he joined the army right after Ryan was born."

"A guy like Jack would never have been happy with a nine-to-five job, you know that. He was too restless. The military was a good fit for him and he knew you and Ryan would be taken care of."

She was prevented from replying when a shadow fell across the table. Holden looked up to see Helen and Brian looking down at them. Kate pulled her hand free from where he still held it in his own.

"I thought that was you, dear," Helen said, before she bent

and pressed a kiss against Kate's cheek. "It's nice to see you getting out. Where is Ryan tonight?"

"He's staying with my mother," Kate replied, smiling at the older woman with genuine affection, before turning her attention to her father-in-law. "Hello, Brian, how are you?"

In his late sixties, Brian Prescott was still a virile man with a trim build and a full head of sandy hair liberally sprinkled with gray. Only his perpetually grumpy expression kept him from being handsome. Holden couldn't recall the last time he'd seen the man smile.

"Doing well. Hello, Holden," he said, extending a stiff hand. "Haven't seen much of you lately. Didn't expect to see you here tonight with my daughter-in-law."

"Hello, Sir." Holden rose to his feet and shook the older man's hand, refusing to feel guilty. "You know Kate and I have been friends since we were kids."

Brian made a grunting sound and turned toward Kate. "I'll be donating another car for the charity raffle this year," he said. "I expect you'll want to be at the kickoff ceremony."

Kate gave Brian a sweet smile. "Actually, I've been thinking it's time I stepped down, but I'm sure Ryan will want to be there with you."

Holden felt a swell of pride in seeing Kate stand up to her former father-in-law, knowing it couldn't have been easy. Brian tucked his chin and Holden didn't miss the flush of dark color that crept up his neck.

"He was your husband and a fallen hero, besides." Brian's voice sounded gravelly with displeasure. "I'd think you'd want to honor his memory."

Kate's serene expression didn't change, but her fingers tightened around her dinner napkin. "I really would like to help, but between working at the diner and baking in the afternoons, I have very little time for anything else. I know you and Ryan will do a great job," she said firmly.

Brian was prevented from answering when Helen laid a gentle hand on his arm. "I think having you and Ryan kick off the raffle is a wonderful idea," she said, looking anxiously at her husband. "There's no reason Kate has to be there, not when she's so busy."

Brian stared at Kate for a moment as if he could will her into compliance, and then blew out a hard breath. "Well, then. Send the boy over one weekend, I have some projects for him."

"I will," Kate promised, her smile still firmly in place.

"Kate, dear, why don't you come over for lunch one day?" Helen glanced at her husband. "There's something Brian and I want to discuss with you."

"Oh." A frown pleated Kate's forehead. "Is everything okay?"

"Yes, nothing to worry about. I'll give you a call and we can set up a date."

"That sounds great," Kate said with a smile, and gave the older woman's fingers a gentle squeeze.

When they were gone, her face fell. She drew in a long breath, before letting it out slowly. She raised wide eyes to Holden. "I can't believe I just said no to Brian."

Holden grinned. "You handled that well."

Kate pulled a face. "He can be a bully sometimes, but deep down he means well. And he adores Ryan, so there's that."

Holden had polished off his own share of the appetizer and now he sat back in his chair and contemplated Kate as she picked at her rollatini. "That's what I remember most about you from high school—you never had a bad word to say about anyone. You were by far the nicest girl in our class."

Kate looked at him in surprise and then a rueful smile

curved her mouth. "I think some people would disagree with you. Nice girls don't get pregnant right after graduation."

Holden had never blamed Kate for getting pregnant. "Jack was a tough guy to say no to. Believe me, I get it."

Kate's eyes twinkled and a small dimple appeared in one cheek. "Oh, did he sweet talk you into bed, too?"

"Very funny. Seriously, though, you were young and very impressionable and he was—"

"He was Jack Prescott, football star and golden boy of Bittersweet Harbor High School," Kate finished. She tipped her head and considered him over the rim of her wine glass. "I always wondered how you two became such good friends."

"Yeah, I'm sure a lot of people wondered about that," Holden said, his tone wry. "The fat kid and the jock. It's like a bad cliché."

Kate looked appalled. "That's not what I meant, Holden Foster, and I wish you would stop referring to yourself that way. I never thought of you as fat. I actually thought you were cool."

"Sure you did," Holden replied, unable to suppress a soft laugh.

"I did!" Kate insisted. "You were always so stoic and quiet. Mysterious, even. And everyone liked you."

"Oh, yeah? What about you, Kate? Did you like me?"

CHAPTER
SEVEN

K ate felt herself go warm beneath Holden's intent gaze, yet she couldn't look away. How would he react if she told him she couldn't stop thinking about how smoking hot he'd looked when he'd answered the door wearing nothing but a pair of unbuttoned blue jeans and a scowl? Or that she was quickly becoming obsessed with his abs, and that his tourmaline brown eyes caused her body to clench in unexpected places? Or that his kiss had literally caused her to go weak in the knees? Even now, he looked virile and attractive in a blue shirt left unbuttoned at the throat, revealing a hint of the snowy white undershirt beneath. In contrast, his skin looked warm and brown and she wondered how it would feel under her lips.

He held his wine glass in one big hand as he regarded her. He could snap the fragile stem with no more than the subtle pressure of his fingers, yet his hold was light. The scattering of small scars across his knuckles reminded her that he was a working man, but she knew how gentle those hands could be. His fingers were long and square-tipped, the nails clean and neatly trimmed. He wore no rings. He'd turned back the cuffs of his shirt, revealing his strong wrists and forearms, the veins prominent beneath his sun-browned skin. She wanted to trace them with her fingertips, feel the warm, vibrant life that pulsed through them.

"I think you know how I feel—how I *felt*," she stammered, incapable of saying more in case he guessed just how much she did like him. More than liked him, if she was being honest with herself. She missed the feel of a man's arms around her, of being kissed and held against a masculine chest. She missed sex, plain and simple, and she hadn't even realized how much until Holden had answered the door in his unbuttoned jeans, looking like every woman's sexy fantasy.

Their food arrived, granting her a short reprieve, but she could see Holden wasn't satisfied with her response. He refilled their wine glasses from the chilled bottle and waited as she took her first bite of tender shrimp.

"Good?"

"Oh, my goodness," she said, nearly moaning in pleasure, "it's amazing. I can't remember the last time I had anything this delicious. How is your puttanesca?"

"Excellent," he acknowledged, and expertly wound more pasta around his fork. "And by the way, I have zero clue as to your feelings, then or now. So maybe you'd like to give me something more specific." He lifted his eyes to her in gentle warning. "And you had better not include the words *grateful* or *friend*. There's only so much bruising a guy's ego can take."

Kate couldn't quite hide a smile. "There should be nothing wrong with your ego, not when beautiful women are sneaking into your bedroom and tearing their clothes off in order to catch your attention."

"I'm not even going to dignify that with a response," he said drily.

"Okay, fine." She gave a helpless laugh. "I don't know what

to say—I didn't really know you when we were in high school. And now—" She broke off, embarrassed. "Let's just say I'm enjoying getting to know you better. How's that?"

"It'll do," he said, still watching her. "For now."

Relieved that he wasn't going to press her further, Kate changed the subject. "How did your meeting with the bank go?"

"Oh, that. It went well. I got approved for a loan to purchase a new lobster boat."

Kate looked at him in surprise. "Really? What about the *Emily Ann*?"

"I'll keep her, for now. She's getting on in years and I decided I need a newer vessel. Tuck is licensed, so he's going to operate the *Emily Ann* and I'll captain the new boat."

"Will you hire a new sternman?"

"Yes, and I'll probably bring on a local kid as an apprentice. I'd offer to take Ryan on for the summer, but somehow I don't think you'd approve."

"Oh, well, it's not that I disapprove," Kate protested weakly. "It's just that he already has a job at the diner. I don't mind him going out with you on occasion, but I can't see him doing it full time."

Ryan bussed tables at the diner during the summer months. The money wasn't bad, but Kate knew he would much rather be out on the water, either sailing his small day skiff on the Nanick River or helping Holden on his lobster boat. She couldn't tell Holden that she worried every time Ryan went out to sea with him because then he would think she didn't trust him to take care of her son. She did, but accidents happened all the time. She knew firsthand how life could change in the space of a heartbeat. She didn't know how she would survive if anything happened to Ryan.

"He'd be safe with me," Holden said, as if reading her thoughts.

"Of course he would," she replied. "And he would love the experience, but if he gets his commercial license he might decide lobstering is more fun than going to college." She gave Holden an earnest look. "I really want him to go to school."

She didn't know how to explain to Holden how important education was to her. She'd been forced to leave college when she'd discovered she was pregnant with Ryan, and Jack had dropped out in order to marry her. She sometimes wondered how different their lives might have been had they both finished school and found good jobs. She'd never regretted her decision to stay home and raise her child, but she often found herself wondering if she'd made a mistake in not finishing her degree. What might she have accomplished? She wanted Ryan to have options that she hadn't had.

"He could do both," Holden said. "I did."

Kate gave him a tolerant look. "Because you're not human. You worked full time on your dad's boat, took night classes at the community college and still managed to purchase and renovate your house on Star Island. And let's not forget all the times you lent me a hand with something. I honestly don't know how you did it."

"Me?" he asked, sounding astonished. "What about you? You worked your ass off at the diner every day, then baked who knows how many cupcakes and pastries each night, all while caring for a baby and holding down the fort while Jack was away. Did you even sleep? C'mon, you're the super hero here, not me."

"I guess when you have no choice, you do what you have to," she said, feeling unaccountably pleased by his praise. "But I had my mom and my sisters to help me with both the baby and the baking, so I actually did manage to get some sleep. But thank you for noticing."

"Like I said, I always noticed."

Something in his voice, an undercurrent of suggestion, made Kate look quickly at him but his expression was inscrutable.

"Well," she finally said, "I don't think Ryan is nearly as driven as either of us were."

"Give him time. He's still figuring things out." He hesitated. "You could still go back, Kate."

"To college?" She gave an uneasy laugh because, as always, he seemed to know her better than she knew herself. "I think that ship sailed a long time ago."

Holden frowned. "You're only thirty-two. There's no time limit on learning. If you'd like, I could show you how I did it, one course at a time. Maybe going back as a full-time student isn't possible, but plenty of people get their degrees through night school." He gave her an encouraging smile. "It's something to think about and it would be a great motivator for Ryan to see his mom going back to school."

"Thank you. I'll think about it. I just want Ryan to have choices, and I really want him to have the full college experience. You know—the dorms, the all-nighters, the dining hall food." She smiled. "The girls."

"And let's not forget the heartbreaks and hangovers," Holden added with a rueful grin. "The second usually caused by the first."

"Did you have your heart broken?" she asked. If Holden had ever been in a serious relationship, she knew nothing about it. Until recently, he'd never shared anything of a personal nature with her.

"Epically," he confessed.

"Really? What happened?" Her curiosity was tinged with an alarming dose of jealousy at the thought of Holden in love.

Holden shrugged. "She found someone else."

"Oh! I'm sorry."

"Don't be. It was a long time ago."

Kate fell silent, wanting badly to ask about the doomed relationship, but Holden's demeanor clearly told her he wouldn't welcome such questions.

"Well," she said after a moment, lifting her wine glass toward him, "here's to broken hearts and fresh starts."

"To new beginnings."

The expression in his steady, dark eyes caused a pleasurable ripple of awareness to chase down her spine. As she took a sip of her wine, she couldn't help hoping a new beginning might actually be possible.

AFTER SHARING a dish of tiramisu paired with a sweet Italian dessert wine, Holden paid the tab and then guided her out of the restaurant and into the cool darkness of the night to where his truck was parked.

"What shall we do now?" he asked, as he handed her into the passenger seat. "It's still early. There's live music at the Breakwater Pub, or we could find somewhere quieter, if you'd like."

Sitting in the passenger seat, Kate was almost on eye-level with Holden as he stood in the open door of the truck, his wide shoulders filling up the space and making her acutely conscious of his height and size. He was close enough that she caught the scent of him, a masculine elixir of woodsy cedar with hints of ginger and clean cotton that sent a sharp, sweet ache of longing through her. No man had a right to smell so good. She wasn't ready to end their evening, but neither did she relish the thought of sitting in a noisy pub.

"I can't stay out too late. I have my morning deliveries to make and I'm working the breakfast shift at the diner. But maybe we could walk along the boardwalk," she suggested, referring to the long stretch of illuminated boardwalk that ran along the Nanick River and afforded views of the harbor and boats. There was a full moon and Kate had always loved the romantic vibe of the waterfront at night.

"Sounds great."

Before she could guess his intent, Holden drew her seatbelt forward and then leaned in to fasten it across her body. Surprised by the unexpected action, Kate drew in a sharp breath and instinctively shrank back to give him more space. As he pulled away, he paused for a moment and their eyes locked. Kate nearly stopped breathing. His gaze drifted over her face, his expression intent. Lifting a hand, he stroked a loose tendril of hair back from her face.

"How long's it been?" Seeing her bemusement, he added, "Since you went on a date?"

"Oh." She tried to gather her scattered thoughts. "A while. I went on a few, a couple of years ago, but they were just coffee dates. This is the first real date I've been on. At night."

His eyes softened. "I'm glad it's with me."

"Yeah," she breathed. "Me, too."

His gaze dropped briefly to her mouth and for just a second she thought he would press his lips to hers. She waited, suspended on a thread of breathless anticipation, but he seemed to recollect himself and he ducked back out of the cab, closing the door firmly between them.

Kate sagged in her seat and expelled a gusty breath. Another second and she might have grabbed him and hauled him close and kissed him the way she'd been imagining doing all night. But when he came around to the driver's side and climbed in beside her, she gave him what she hoped was a friendly smile while her insides felt like a mini cyclone had been unleashed.

They found a parking spot near the harbor and made their

way across the grassy lawn of Harborside Park toward the boardwalk. The park was softly lit by vintage-style gas lights, and couples strolled together or in small groups beneath the spreading boughs of the trees. The moon cast a buttery reflection on the water and the haunting strains of a violin carried on the warm breeze, as a busker played beneath a street lamp. They paused to listen for a few minutes before Holden withdrew his wallet and dropped several bills into the open violin case on the ground in front of the man. The musician nodded his thanks and Holden took Kate's hand as they continued to walk. The casual contact caused Kate's heart to thump unsteadily. His hand was warm and dry and his fingers closed strongly around her own. As if sensing her sudden discomposure, he glanced at her.

"Doing okay?"

"Yes." Her voice came out breathless. "I love the waterfront at night."

"It is beautiful," he agreed, but something in his tone caused Kate to look at him, only to find him watching her and not the water. The heat in his dark eyes caused an involuntary shiver of desire to run through her. Holden frowned and drew her to a stop. "Cold? Come here."

He drew her against the hard warmth of his body and his arms closed around her. They stood in the violet shadows between two lamp poles, but Kate was acutely aware of other people walking past them on the boardwalk. For just an instant she resisted, but Holden smelled incredible and he was so warm that she instinctively inched closer. He skated one big hand along her spine and settled it between her shoulder blades where he rubbed soothing circles against her back. With her face pressed against his shoulder, she could feel the steady rise and fall of his chest and the press of hard muscles beneath the cotton shirt. She knew she should push him away, but instead she slid her arms around his waist, seeking more of the delicious contact.

"Kate..." His warm breath fanned her cheek.

Without conscious thought, she raised her face to his and her lips parted in invitation. With a soft groan, Holden eased his mouth over hers as one hand came up to cradle the nape of her neck and tilt her head back. The kiss was slow and searching as he explored the contours of her lips, sending bolts of pleasure through her. She made in inarticulate sound of encouragement and he delved deeper, opening her mouth and sinking his tongue inside. The taste and heat of him was intoxicating, drowning her in sensation and making her shiver and press closer. He angled his mouth over hers, sweeping his tongue against hers in hot, silken passes. She felt drugged by the sheer potency of him. She didn't know how long the kiss went on, but when he finally lifted his head, Kate sagged against him, all the strength leached from her limbs. Her breath came in soft gusts and her fingers fisted in the fabric of his shirt. She felt overwhelmed and woozy, as if she'd sprinted up eight flights of stairs, or guzzled a bottle of champagne. Holden kept his arms around her, supporting her, until she found the energy to put some space between them. Even then, he didn't let her go, not completely. He kept one hand at the curve of her waist while he caressed the side of her face with the back of his fingers.

"I've been wanting to do that for a while," he said in a low voice.

Kate shook her head, bemused. "I didn't know, you never let on."

"The timing wasn't right."

They were close enough that even in the indistinct light she could see the beginnings of beard shadow on his face. How would that masculine stubble feel against the tender skin of her neck? Against other parts of her body? The urge to rub her fingertips over his lean jaw was so strong that she took a step back.

Holden let his hands fall to his sides, but his eyes remained locked with hers, his expression inscrutable. Kate wrapped her arms around her middle and they continued to walk slowly along the boardwalk. Her mind was in a whirl, wondering how she could have missed the signs. She wasn't obtuse. If Holden had given any indication he found her attractive, she would have known. Wouldn't she? But he'd remained infuriatingly reserved every time he'd come by to check on her.

"How long, exactly?" she asked.

"What?"

"How long have you wanted to do that? Kiss me?"

"Ah, Kate…" A low, rueful laugh escaped him. The deliciously masculine sound slid across her already heightened senses like a physical caress. "I don't know. A while."

"But—"

"Don't try to analyze it."

"I wasn't," she fibbed. "I just wondered if this is something new for you, or—"

"It's not new. Like I said, the timing wasn't right."

"But it is now?"

"I think so, yes."

They had reached the far end of the boardwalk and Holden drew her down onto a nearby bench. He leaned back and stretched one arm along the bench behind her. She leaned into him and could feel the heat that radiated from his big frame. A commercial party boat made its way through the harbor. The upper deck was strung with multi-colored lights and Kate could see a crowd of people dancing to the music that swelled from the onboard speakers.

"Look," Kate said, pointing beyond the party boat to the far side of the harbor. "You can see my parents' house."

At one end of Scanty Island was the All Shook Up Diner. At the easternmost point of the small island stood the Belshaw family home. From where they sat, both the island and the house looked small. Kate could just make out the small dock where Ryan kept his day sailboat.

"Someone's at home," Holden observed. "The lights are on."

"Probably Erin or my mother. I don't think Savannah spends much time there anymore, at least not according to Erin."

"When are she and Jed getting married?"

"The weekend after Labor Day." She paused for a moment as an idea occurred to her. "Maybe you could be my plus-one."

Holden looked at her in surprise. "Your what?"

Kate couldn't meet his eyes, instead pretending interest in the people who strolled by. Butterflies rioted in her stomach. Asking Holden to be her date at her sister's wedding implied a relationship they weren't even close to having. Summer hadn't yet begun, not officially. Labor Day was still months away. The only reason her sister had even given her the option of bringing someone to the wedding was because she lived in hopeful anticipation that Kate might find someone she liked enough to bring along.

And she had.

"My date," she clarified. "To the wedding. If you want to, that is."

"Surely you're a bridesmaid," Holden said. "Won't you be paired with a groomsman?"

"Only for the ceremony. I'm still allowed to bring someone," Kate told him. "There's no head table since they've decided to do passed appetizers and food stations in lieu of a sit-down meal. So aside from the ceremony and photos, I'm just like any other guest."

"Sure, I'm all in." His acceptance was immediate, as if he

had no worries about how their relationship might develop over the course of the summer. "In fact, I look forward to it."

"Okay, good." She drew in a deep breath, both relieved and anxious about his ready committal to escort her to what would be a very large, very public event. Her sister, Savannah, was marrying Jed Lawson, after all, the only son of Mason and Clarissa Lawson, arguably the wealthiest and most influential people in Bittersweet Harbor. Everyone who was anyone would be at the wedding. People would draw conclusions—right or wrong—when they saw Kate and Holden together. Was she ready for that?

She honestly didn't know.

CHAPTER
EIGHT

K ate was happy to see all four of her sisters at the family house on Scanty Island when she and Ryan arrived the following day. While both Erin and Savannah worked with her at the diner, she didn't see either Maggie or Rowan nearly as much as she would have liked. Now she helped her mother lay out place settings on the long kitchen table while Savannah poured glasses of wine, Rowan tossed together a salad, and Erin put the finishing touches to the pan-seared scallops and lemon-asparagus risotto she had cooked.

"That smells amazing," Maggie said, as she leaned back against the counter with her glass of wine and watched Erin cook. She wore a black tee shirt with the name of her motorcycle shop across the back, and her colorful arm tattoos were on full display. "You make it look so easy."

Erin grinned at her sister. "It is easy. You should try it sometime."

Maggie gave her sister a wry look. "Have you tasted my cooking?"

"Maggie would rather order takeout for every meal than

cook her own food," Rowan declared, as she placed the salad bowl on the table. "With all the sodium and trans fats you consume, it's a wonder you're still alive."

"Ha. This, from the woman who only eats salads," Maggie said, without rancor. "No wonder you're so scrawny."

Rowan tucked a strand of dark hair behind one ear and gave Maggie an amused look. "It's called healthy. And in case you forgot, I do eat seafood, smarty pants."

Maggie pursed her lips and considered Rowan thoughtfully. "Yeah, I don't get it. You work at the seacoast center and teach kids about marine life, and yet you have no compunctions about eating the very creatures you want to save."

Rowan had majored in marine biology in college. When she wasn't working at the Seacoast Science Center, she ran an eco-tour boat on the Nanick River and through the estuaries behind Star Island, educating the public about local marine and wildlife.

"I only eat sustainable seafood," she said now. "Those scallops are farm-raised, so there's minimal impact on the marine environment."

"Okay, girls, enough of that. Let's eat," Erin said, setting the scallops and rice on the table. "Kate, why don't you give Ryan a shout? He's down at the dock."

While the others took their seats, Kate stepped onto the wide, covered porch and looked to where Ryan was sitting on his small sailboat, absorbed in looking at his phone. "Ryan, dinner is ready."

Her son stepped onto the dock and then jogged the short distance to the porch. He was growing faster than she could keep up with. He looked very much like his father, but where Jack had been athletic and solidly built, Ryan was long-limbed and coltish. He had an insatiable appetite, but he had yet to fill out. God help the girls when he did. Now he bounded up the steps to join her on the porch.

"What're we having?" he asked.

"Scallops and asparagus risotto. No, don't roll your eyes. Erin's worked hard putting the meal together."

"I'd rather have a burger."

Kate steered him toward the door. "I brought peanut butter cookies and a chocolate cake for dessert, but if you're still hungry when we get home I'll cook you a burger. I promise." She took a seat between her mother and Ryan, and waited as the dishes were passed around the table. "Are you all set for the wedding?" she asked Savannah.

"I think so. I have a final dress fitting in August, and that's it. Thank you so much for agreeing to make the wedding cake."

"Thank you for trusting me to make it," Kate said, smiling. "I won't let you down."

In reality, she had been anxious about baking the cake, a five-tiered lemon and blueberry cake with a classic white frosting, adorned with ornate piping and natural greenery. She'd been experimenting with different batters for weeks in an attempt to find the perfect flavor profile.

"The one thing I insisted on was that you make the cake. Once the final dress fitting is complete, all I have to do is show up. Honestly, I'll be glad when it's all over. I would much rather have eloped." Savannah sighed and tucked a strand of bright auburn hair behind her ear. "I know my future mother-in-law means well, but she has an opinion about *everything*."

"Well, you can't blame her. Jed is her only son," Pauline said in a reasonable tone.

"Really, Mom?" Savannah asked in bewilderment. "You're defending her?"

Clarissa Lawson nee Hayes had grown up in Bittersweet

95

Harbor and had dated Mike Belshaw in high school. But when Pauline had moved into town one summer, he had ditched Clarissa and begun dating Pauline instead, before marrying her the summer after she'd graduated from high school. Clarissa had harbored a decades-long grudge toward both Mike and Pauline, which extended to the five Belshaw daughters, as well. Only when Jed had announced he would marry Savannah had she begun to let go of her resentment. While not exactly warm and friendly, Clarissa was at least civil and seemed to want the best for her son and future daughter-in-law. She had even pulled strings to reserve the coveted Davenport Yacht Club for the wedding venue, when it was typically booked two years in advance.

"But isn't it the bride's prerogative to do what she wants for her own wedding?" Erin asked. "Besides, Clarissa has a daughter. Let her throw her weight around when Kyla gets married."

"Yeah, that's a big *if* Kyla gets married," Savannah said with a smirk. "Let's face it, who would be brave enough to take her on?"

There was general laughter as they agreed with Savannah's assessment of Kyla Lawson, who was beautiful, but as snobbish as her mother.

"Speaking of the wedding," Kate said casually, as she spooned a generous helping of risotto onto her plate, "I've invited someone to come with me."

The remnants of laughter abruptly stopped as her family stared at her in surprise.

"Wow. That's great!" Savannah finally said. "Who is it?"

"Holden," Ryan volunteered, as he speared a golden scallop with his fork. "They even went on a date last night."

Pauline turned to look at her oldest daughter with wide eyes. "You didn't tell me you had a *date*."

"Holden Foster?" Maggie asked, incredulous. "The fat kid from high school?"

96

"Please don't say that," Kate admonished, appalled that anyone would characterize Holden that way when he had so many amazing attributes beyond his looks which, by the way, were also amazing. "He looks great, but even if he was overweight, it wouldn't matter to me."

Ryan was laughing at the idea of anyone calling Holden fat, and both Rowan and Savannah talked over each other in their haste to assure Maggie that not only wasn't Holden Foster fat, he was *hot*.

"You've been gone for ten years," Erin said, leaning forward to look at Maggie. "Holden may have been heavy as a teenager, but trust me when I say you wouldn't recognize him now. Rowan is right—the guy is serious eye candy."

Maggie put both hands up in surrender. "Okay, sorry. I haven't seen him in ten years so how would I know? What's he doing these days?"

"He's a lobsterman," Kate said.

"Of course he is." Maggie's voice dripped with disdain.

An uncomfortable silence descended on the table as they each recalled the reasons why Maggie had left Bittersweet Harbor more than ten years ago. She and Colton Rush, an apprentice lobsterman, had been crazy about each other all through high school and the years following graduation, but some disagreement had caused them to briefly split up. After spending a miserable summer apart, they had finally patched things up and gotten back together, and had even made plans to move in together when local bad girl, Cheyenne Jarrett, had come forward, claiming she was pregnant with Colton's baby. Colton hadn't denied it. Instead, he'd married Cheyenne, determined to make a go of their relationship while a heartbroken Maggie had fled to Florida.

"Holden isn't Colton," Kate said quietly.

Maggie blew out a hard breath. "I'm sorry. I guess I haven't been away long enough if I can be triggered by the word *lobsterman*."

"It's okay," Rowan said, reaching out to squeeze Maggie's hand. "We're all just happy to have you back. He doesn't live around here anymore, so at least you don't need to worry about running into him. But if you want me to hunt him down and break his kneecaps, just say the word."

"Thanks, hon," Maggie said, and gave Rowan a brief, one-armed hug.

"So tell us all about the date," Erin urged, changing the subject. "Where did you go?"

"He took me to Luigi's, which was gorgeous and the food was delicious." Kate cast a swift glance at Ryan, keeping her tone light and upbeat. "And we ran into Brian and Helen, who were also having dinner there."

"Isn't that special," Erin murmured, before lifting her wine-glass to her mouth.

"Well, it's not like you and Holden haven't known each other forever," Pauline said. "They can hardly expect you to live like a nun."

Ryan gave a snort of laughter. "I don't think Mom could be a nun. I saw her kiss him."

Kate rounded on her son with a look of astonishment. "Ryan Prescott, you never did!"

But Ryan just grinned into his glass of lemonade while his aunts each struggled to hide their own surprised smiles.

"So you like him?" Rowan asked. "He seems really nice. You know he lives right down the road from me, right? He has a really nice place."

There was no way Kate would tell her sisters about her disastrous visit to Holden's house. They would never let her live it down and she didn't want to cast his younger sister or her college friend in a bad light.

"Of course I like him. He was a good friend of Jack's," Kate said, hoping none of her sisters saw through her affected nonchalance to her true feelings. She ruffled Ryan's hair. "And he always looked out for us whenever your dad was away, didn't he? He still does." Glancing around the table, she saw the knowing expressions on each of her sisters' faces. "What? He's just a friend!"

But the words didn't ring true, even to her own ears.

"I've seen the way he looks at you," Savannah said. "You should go for it."

Kate flushed. If her sisters could have seen her the previous night on the boardwalk, locked in Holden's arms, they might conclude she had already gone for it.

"Will you go out with him again?" Rowan asked.

"He hasn't asked, but maybe," Kate demurred, sliding a cautious look at Ryan.

Her son shrugged. "I don't mind."

"I always liked Holden," Pauline said. "He seems to have his priorities straight. I think it would be nice if the two of you started dating. You're still young and you've been alone for too long."

"Okay," Kate said briskly, desperate to change the subject, "who wants to hear about my trip to New York City?"

For the next hour, as they finished dinner and lingered over coffee and dessert, they talked and laughed and shared stories, until finally Kate announced it was time for her and Ryan to head home.

"He has school tomorrow and I'm not sure he's finished all his homework," she said, giving Ryan a meaningful look.

"Fine," he grumbled, and gathered his things.

"Don't forget next weekend is Memorial Day," Savannah said. "We're bringing Dad home on Monday for the family barbeque. You should invite Holden."

"I'll think about it," Kate promised. "But even if I don't bring him, I'll definitely bring dessert."

Kate hugged each of her sisters, and her mother walked with her to the porch. The full moon was just beginning to rise over the horizon, reminding her again of her evening with Holden.

"Kate," her mother said softly, putting a hand on her arm and preventing her from heading down the steps.

Seeing her mother's expression, Kate looked at Ryan. "Go on ahead, sweetie. I'll catch up." She waited until her son was out of earshot. "What is it?"

"I just want to say I'm glad you're dating. You were a good wife and you're a wonderful mother, but now it's time to think about yourself and what *you* want." She cupped Kate's face in her cool hands and smiled gently. "I meant it when I said I've always liked Holden. He's a man you can rely on."

Kate knew her mother's words were a not-so-subtle dig at Jack. Pauline believed Jack had abandoned Kate and Ryan when they'd needed him most. Maybe she was right, but Kate didn't want to argue the point with her mother. Jack was gone. Whatever his shortcomings had been no longer mattered.

"Thanks for dinner, Mom. I'll see you later."

As she and Ryan drove home, Ryan turned in his seat to look at her. "What did Gram mean when she said Holden has his priorities straight?"

Kate fixed her eyes on the road. "Well, he's a hard worker. He has his own house and his own business and he's the kind of man people trust." She glanced at her son. "More importantly, he cares about other people."

"Like us?"

"Yes, I think so."

Ryan was quiet for a moment. "Do you like him?"

Kate glanced at her son. "Of course. I've known him for most of my life."

"I know that," Ryan replied, sounding aggrieved. "But do you *like* like him?"

Kate chewed her lip, wondering how to respond. She knew Ryan enjoyed Holden's company, but did he worry about being supplanted in her affection by another guy? "Listen," she said after a moment, "I do like Holden, but I want you to know he could never, *ever* replace you in my heart. You know that, right?"

"Mom," he groaned, "I'm not worried about that. I just think if you guys like each other, you should go out with him."

"You wouldn't mind?"

"Nope. And maybe then you'd let me go on his boat more."

"Aha," Kate said, smiling. "I knew there was an ulterior motive."

Ryan laughed, but then grew sober. "Seriously, Mom, if he asks you out again, say yes. I know you're going to the wedding with him, but you should definitely do stuff with him before that."

"Why the sudden interest in me dating?"

"I dunno." He shrugged. "You just seem happy lately, and I like that."

As Kate turned onto their street and pulled the van into the driveway of their small townhouse, she acknowledged Ryan was right. She *was* happy, and it was all because of Holden Foster.

CHAPTER
NINE

Holden was a firm believer in striking while the iron was hot. He hadn't yet asked Kate for a second date, not wanting to scare her off, but he did want her thinking about him and their night together. On Monday, after returning from a day at sea, he drove to Petals and Posies, a local florist and nursery. He wandered through the fragrant flower shop and tried to decide what Kate might like, when an older woman approached him.

"Can I help you?" Her face was tanned and seamed with wrinkles, but her blue eyes were lively and friendly. "I'm Caroline."

"Hi," he replied. "I'm Holden. Are you the owner?"

"Once upon a time," she confirmed, "but now my daughter, Lily, runs the place. I just come in a few days a week to help out."

Holden grinned. "Lily, huh?"

The woman's smile grew broader. "What can I say? I love flowers. Now how can I help you?"

"I want to send flowers to someone, but I've no idea what she might like."

"Is she a family member or a friend?"

"Definitely a friend, but I'm working on becoming more."

"I understand," smiled the woman. "Does she know how you feel?"

Holden thought again about the kiss they'd shared on the boardwalk. "I think she's beginning to realize."

"What about roses? They're lovely and there's no mistaking their meaning."

Holden hesitated. "Aren't they a little obvious? I'd like something special, maybe more subtle."

"Of course. Come with me, I have an idea." Holden followed her through the flower shop to a room where dozens of vases of cut flowers and greenery were on display in a row of glass-fronted coolers. A long work table stood nearby, with rolls of florist tape and colorful ribbon on the wall. "Do you have a color preference?"

Holden shrugged. "Not really, but I know she likes purple and pink."

"Let me put something together for you," Caroline suggested. "If you don't like it, you're under no obligation to buy it. But I promise you, she will love it."

If Holden didn't know better he'd think the woman was up to something, but her expression was guileless as she waited for his response. After a moment, he nodded. "That sounds good. Thank you."

"Excellent. Give me fifteen minutes."

Holden wandered through the flower shop, pausing to look at the many little gifts on display without really seeing them. He'd never sent flowers to a woman before and now he wondered if he was overdoing it. But this was Kate. When was the last time anyone had sent her flowers? Maybe not since Jack had died. If anyone deserved flowers, Kate did. When twenty minutes had passed, he went back to where Caroline was putting the finishing touches on a stunning bouquet in varying shades of lavender, purple, pink, and white, accented with delicate greenery.

"What do you think?" Caroline asked. She had placed the flowers in a clear, slender vase that almost looked too fragile to hold the dense bouquet.

"I think it looks amazing," he replied honestly. "Is that vase sturdy enough?"

"Oh, yes, but we'll place it in a supporting box for transport." Caroline paused. "Are you hand-carrying this to her, or would you like us to deliver it?"

Retrieving his wallet, Holden considered the question. "Delivery, please."

"Would you like to include a card? We have some here," she said, indicating a small display of note cards. He chose one and after a moment, simply scrawled his name.

While he paid for the flowers and provided Kate's address, a young woman appeared from a back room and deftly secured the vase in a white cardboard base. She gave Holden a friendly smile.

"This is my daughter, Lily."

"Nice to meet you," Holden said. "Okay, I think that about does it. When will she receive the flowers?"

Caroline glanced at the large clock on the wall. "Our last deliveries go out in an hour, so these should be delivered by six o'clock."

"Perfect. Thanks very much for your help." He nodded to the younger woman and left the shop.

CAROLINE DRUMLIN CLEARED AWAY the leftover bits of flower stems and ribbon from the work table, feeling quite pleased with herself. Lily looked at her mother with narrowed eyes. "I know that look in your eyes. What are you up to?"

Caroline gave a satisfied smile and carried the bouquet over to the cooler where it would remain until the delivery van was ready to depart. "A little birdie told me Holden Foster went out Saturday night with Kate Prescott."

"And?"

"And since Kate is the daughter of a very dear friend of mine and since I happen to believe she deserves a chance at happiness, I thought I might help things along a bit."

Lily looked puzzled. "How?"

"Kate Prescott has taken three of our classes on the secret language of flowers and the hidden meaning of bouquets. She comes in here quite often." She gave her daughter a meaningful look. "She understands flowers."

"Oh." Lily's eyes drifted to the bouquet in the cooler and her eyes widened in sudden comprehension. "Oh!"

"Exactly," Caroline murmured, and she and her daughter shared a knowing smile.

KATE ESPECIALLY LIKED Mondays because the diner was closed and she didn't make deliveries to the local coffee shops or B&Bs. It was her day to do whatever she liked and today she was making French macarons, using the techniques she had learned from Paul Bellecourt during his master class. The elegant sandwich cookies looked deceptively simple, but Kate had discovered they were challenging to make. She was on her fifth batch and she thought she'd finally mastered the little darlings. Batches of lemon, pistachio, chocolate and raspberry flavored macarons, in delicate pastel shades, were stacked neatly on a nearby tray. She was mixing up some buttercream frosting for the last bunch when her front doorbell rang. Glancing at the clock she saw it was just past six o'clock. She'd completely lost track of time, had promised Ryan she would pick him up at her mother's house at five, as he had wanted to take his sailboat out. She was already late and now she had a visitor.

Wiping her hands on a dish towel, she walked through the apartment and opened the front door to see a young man holding a beautiful floral arrangement.

"Kate Prescott?" he asked.

"Yes."

"Delivery for you." Pushing the bouquet into her hands, he retreated down the front steps and strode to a white van parked at the curb with the *Petals and Posies* logo emblazoned on the side. Kate stood for a moment in the doorway, admiring the blooms. As she turned to go back into the house, Erin's car pulled up and Ryan climbed out of the passenger side.

"I was just coming to get you," Kate called. "Honest!"

"Sure, Mom." He paused to admire the flowers. "Who're those from? As if I need to ask."

Erin followed Ryan up the walkway, eyeing the flowers. "Wow, those are gorgeous. I'm guessing they're from Holden?"

"I don't know," Kate admitted, but hoped Erin was right. She carried the flowers into the kitchen and set them on the table before pulling the small card from the plastic display stick. "Yes, they're from Holden. That's so sweet of him."

"What does the card say?"

Kate turned it over in her hands. "Nothing, just his name."

"Did something happen between the two of you?" Erin asked, moving along the counter to better study the macarons on display. "Because in my experience, guys only send flowers for two reasons."

Kate placed the small card next to the floral arrangement. "And what are those?"

Erin selected a pale yellow macaron before answering. "Either he's done something incredibly stupid and flowers are his way of apologizing, or..." She bit into the delicate cookie and her eyes closed on a soft moan of pleasure. "Oh, these are amazing."

Kate glanced around to ensure Ryan wasn't within earshot. "Or what?"

"Or he had the best sex of his life and wants to show his appreciation," Erin said, waggling her eyebrows suggestively. "So which is it?"

Grabbing a nearby hand towel, Kate snapped it against her younger sister's leg, laughing in spite of herself. "Neither!"

"But you can't tell me you haven't thought about it," Erin said slyly. "I mean, c'mon, the guy is hot and single and obviously into you."

Kate flushed even as the words filled her with pleasure, but there was no way she could tell Erin just how much she *had* thought about it, or how her imagination had suddenly become her own private, big-screen viewing room, filled with explicit images of what it might be like to be intimate with Holden, to have those strong hands on her body, caressing her...

"We kissed," she admitted, "but that's it. And if he's so into me, why has he waited this long to ask me out?"

"For obvious reasons. You'd lost your husband, who just happened to be his best friend. I'm sure he's had all sorts of conflicted feelings about starting a relationship with you. Maybe he wanted to make sure your head was in the right place. Everyone knows rebound romances never work out."

Kate looked at her sister, surprised. "Do you think that's what he wants? A relationship?" She glanced again at the bouquet and any further words died. The beautiful arrangement boasted a dozen different types of flowers, including pink camellias and deep purple heliotrope, white gardenias and sweet William.

Surely it had to be coincidence. There was no way Holden could know the symbolism behind the flowers he'd sent, and yet they seemed specific in the message they conveyed. A message that made her heart thud harder and her legs feel a little weak.

Oblivious to Kate's sudden distraction, Erin shrugged and snagged a second macaron. "What else? C'mon, Kate, even you can't be that naïve. The guy has been coming by here since Ryan was a baby, doing all the things a husband would do while your own husband was deployed on the other side of the world."

Not all the things.

"He never crossed a line," she said stiffly. "In fact, I always believed he must have made some sort of promise to Jack to take care of us whenever Jack was away. He never once gave any indication that he might have feelings for me." She paused, and then added for good measure, "Nothing ever happened between us."

"Of course not," Erin said hastily, and came around the counter to hug Kate. "That thought never even occurred to me. I mean, look at you!"

Kate pulled out of Erin's arms and scowled at her, suddenly conscious of her untidy appearance. Her hair was pulled back in a messy ponytail and her apron had smears of macaron ingredients across the front. "What's that supposed to mean?"

"*Nothing.* Just that you've always been the nice sister, the *good* sister—the one who would never do or say anything bad."

"And I suppose getting pregnant right after high school doesn't count?"

Erin pulled a face. "Honestly, I think that says more about Jack than it does about you. That guy could charm the panties off a nun." Then, seeing Kate's expression, hurried to add, "Not that you're at all like a nun, which I think we established yesterday at dinner."

Kate's gaze slid again to the bouquet on the table. "It was just a kiss, Erin. No big deal."

Liar.

Erin considered Kate thoughtfully. "If you like him, Kate, then tell him. Holden strikes me as the kind of guy who would never push himself forward. You can't blame him. It couldn't have been easy for him in high school, being Jack's best friend and looking the way he did."

Kate only barely resisted rolling her eyes. "Why does everyone keep harping on what he looked like in high school? That was so long ago! Besides, he doesn't strike me as a person with low self-esteem."

"I'm just saying he might need some encouragement. Look how long it's taken him to ask you out." She put a hand on Kate's arm. "He's a great guy and he would never lead you on, which makes me think this date might have been a big deal for him. But if you want him, make sure he knows. Don't be afraid to make the first move. You're a grown woman with a kid for Pete's sake. Own it."

"So I should what—be the aggressor?"

She'd made the comment sarcastically, but Erin only shrugged. "Why not? It would probably be empowering for both of you. When's the last time you got laid?" Seeing Kate's expression, she laughed. "C'mon, you know you want to, and it would be good for you."

"You're impossible," Kate spluttered, but seeing Erin's grin, she couldn't suppress her own laughter. "Okay, I'll think about it."

"You already are!" Erin sang out as she made her way toward the door. "I'll see you tomorrow."

After she had gone, Kate sat down at the table and stared at Holden's bouquet. She couldn't remember the meaning of every flower, but she recalled enough from the series of classes she'd taken about the secret language of flowers to wonder if the selection of blooms had been deliberate. Pink camellia meant *longing for you*. Purple heliotrope meant *devotion*. And everyone knew gardenias were code for *secret love*.

But did she really believe Holden understood the language of flowers and was using them to declare his secret, undying love for her? His specialty was lobsters and woodworking, not flowers. And yet she couldn't deny she was both intrigued and charmed by the idea. Just the fact he'd been thoughtful enough to send flowers was enough. She'd never received flowers from a man, not even Jack, whose idea of a romantic gesture had been to bring home a meat-lover's pizza with two or three slices missing because he'd been too hungry to wait until he got home to eat.

Now she plucked a single gardenia stem from the vase and brought it to her nose and breathed in the sweet, tropical fragrance. Maybe Erin was right. Maybe she needed to become more assertive. She closed her eyes and thought again of how incredibly sexy Holden had looked when he'd answered the door, half naked and wet. She simply couldn't get that image out of her head. She recalled the way his expression had turned all intent and dangerous when he'd chased her back to her house to tell her he hadn't been having sex with another woman. Just the memory made her go hot and shivery all over. Was she one of those women who secretly thrilled to overtly masculine, aggressive men? She didn't think so, but she acknowledged Holden's forceful attitude had been more than a little stirring. What would it be like to have a man like that take you to bed? She knew instinctively it would be good—better than good.

She stroked the soft petals of the flower across her lips, remembering the kiss they'd shared on the boardwalk. That kiss had been hot. Needy. Unlike any other kiss she'd experienced.

Ever.

Jack had not been a kisser, preferring to get to the *good stuff* as quickly as possible. For him, kissing had been something he did only as a necessary prelude to the main attraction, and even that had often felt rushed and unsatisfying. In contrast, Holden had taken his time, kissing her slowly and thoroughly, as if there were nothing else he wanted or needed to do. If he was that good at kissing, what would the sex be like? She covered her hot face with her hands and gave a shaky laugh because she couldn't stop thinking about it.

Erin's words replayed in her head; *it would be good for you.*

Was she ready to take that kind of step? She knew Erin was right when she'd said Holden would never lead her on. If she was going to encourage him she needed to be all in, because she instinctively understood he wasn't the kind of guy who played games. It actually made sense that he might have been holding back because of some loyalty he felt toward Jack. Five years after his death, she still worried that people would judge her if she became romantically involved with someone. But even Holden had told her she shouldn't be alone. Maybe her mother was right—life was short and maybe it was time she began thinking about what *she* wanted. And against all reason, she wanted Holden Foster.

CHAPTER
TEN

K ate didn't hear from Holden on Tuesday or Wednesday, and went to work at the diner on Thursday feeling restless and out of sorts. She'd left a message on his phone on Tuesday, thanking him for the flowers and ending the message with an awkward *Hope to see you soon!* But there had been nothing but deafening silence in return. She'd risked calling him again on Wednesday afternoon but when the call went directly to voicemail, she'd quickly hung up without saying anything.

She hadn't really dated as an adult and she wasn't sure about the rules. Did a single date—a single kiss—even qualify as *dating*? She felt out of her depth, as uncertain and anxious as an adolescent. Whenever her phone did buzz, she had a surge of anticipation but none of the callers were Holden. She knew there was a logical explanation for his silence. He wasn't the sort of person who would deliberately ignore her calls. Even so, she couldn't help feeling worried, wondering if she had only imagined the chemistry they'd shared on the boardwalk. For the past two days, she'd thrown herself into baking her pastries and desserts to keep herself busy and her mind occupied, had visited her father every day at the nursing home, and had twice driven past Holden's house on Star Island on the pretext of visiting her sister, Rowan, but his truck had been conspicuously absent.

Today she'd woken up at five a.m., had made her morning deliveries to the coffee shops and inns, and was three hours into the morning breakfast rush at the diner when she spotted Emily Foster and her friend, Sam, slide into a vacant booth.

"I'll take this one," she said to Savannah. If she was serious about encouraging Holden—about becoming *involved* with him —her first order of business was to assess the competition. Holden might say he wasn't interested in Emily's friend, but that didn't mean the coed wasn't still interested in him. After quickly checking that her hair was in order, she drew in a deep breath and approached the booth, smiling at Emily and then swiftly appraising the other girl who was perusing the menu, her face hidden behind a curtain of honey blonde hair. "Good morning, ladies. Can I bring you coffee or something to drink?"

Sam glanced up and Kate felt her stomach plummet. The girl was drop dead gorgeous, with swimming pool blue eyes, a lush, pink mouth and sun-kissed skin that glowed with the vitality of youth and good health. *This* was the woman Holden had walked away from? Kate suddenly felt ages older than her thirty-two years, and knew she probably looked as haggard and frumpy as she suddenly felt.

"I'll have a cranberry juice," Sam said. "And an iced coffee. Do you have cold brew?"

"No, just plain old iced coffee," Kate said sweetly.

"Okay, I guess I'll have a plain old iced coffee with oat milk and no sugar."

Kate turned her attention to Emily who gave her a friendly smile. "Hi Kate. I'll have the regular hot coffee, please, and a glass of orange juice."

"You got it."

She turned away and slid behind the long breakfast counter to pour the juice, but not before she heard Emily say, "She's the one I told you about—the widow that Holden takes care of."

Kate slid a sidelong glance at the table as she filled the glasses. The two girls were leaning across the table toward each other, trying to keep their voices down, but they were audible even above the clink of dishware and the hum of conversation.

"That's her?" Sam's voice held a note of surprise. "I thought she'd be older."

"I told you she's Holden's age."

"She looks a lot younger. Do you think he likes her?"

But Emily only had time to shrug and then lean back as Kate brought them their coffee and juice. "Have you decided what you'd like to eat? Our specials are on the board over the counter."

After taking their orders, Kate paused, looking at Sam. "You're Emily's friend from college, right? I almost didn't recognize you."

With your clothes on.

She sensed Sam's surprise; could almost see the wheels turning in her pretty head as she tried to figure out how Kate might know her.

"Um, yeah, I'm Samantha but everyone just calls me Sam. Have we met?"

"Well, not officially."

"She's staying with me for the summer," Emily offered. "We're working at the Flybridge."

"That must be fun," Kate said, smiling. "I'll bet you spend a lot of time at the beach when you're not working, am I right? I'm guessing that was your Prius I saw parked at your brother's house last week?"

Kate didn't miss the look the girls exchanged, or the sudden, cautious awareness in Sam's blue eyes.

"Yes, that's my car," Emily said. "Did you come by?"

"I did, actually, but I didn't stay because Holden was trying to get rid of one of those annoying door-to-door solicitors."

"Oh, I hate when they come around," Emily groaned. "They *are* annoying. What was the guy trying to sell?"

"Oh, it was a woman," Kate said, holding Sam's gaze for a brief instant. "Whatever she was selling, Holden had no interest in buying. He looked *very* annoyed," Kate said cheerfully.

She caught Sam's dismayed expression and for just an instant she felt a pang of sympathy for the younger woman. Holden's rejection had to have stung, and now Sam knew that Kate knew what had happened. That had to sting even worse. But she needed Sam to understand that Holden was off-limits.

He was *hers*.

The thought was so startling that she almost didn't hear Emily's question. "I'm sorry, what did you say?"

Emily was looking at her with a mixture of dawning awareness and amusement. "Are you and my brother *dating*?"

She thought again of the kiss she'd shared with Holden on the boardwalk, and allowed a slow smile to spread across her face. "Yeah, as matter of fact we are. Well, enough chatting—I'll get your order in right away."

She included both girls in her smile, but Sam had her face buried in her iced coffee with her hair hanging forward, obscuring her expression. Turning away, Kate felt an absurd satisfaction in having let the younger woman know where she stood. At the same time, her pulse skittered erratically because she had actually confirmed—*to Holden's sister*—that she and Holden were a thing, which suddenly made it seem real. She didn't know who had been more surprised by her announcement—Emily or herself. But she also felt a lightness she hadn't experienced in years. When was the last time she had actually felt excited about a guy? Maybe not since high school when Jack had pursued her with a single-minded intensity, charming her right out of her sensible, cotton panties.

She didn't engage either of the two girls in conversation again except to bring them their food and then their check, despite the curious glances Emily cast her way. Kate was dying to ask her if she'd seen Holden recently, but that would have alerted Sam that she wasn't as cozy with Holden as she had implied. After they left, the lunch shift went swiftly and finally it was time to clean up and close the diner.

"So when will you see Holden again?" Erin asked, as they moved from table to table on the outside deck, closing umbrellas.

"I don't know," Kate admitted. "I haven't heard from him since he sent me the flowers. I left him a voicemail but he hasn't called back. Maybe I should try him again."

"Or drop by his house tonight with a bottle of wine and a plate of your famous brownies," Erin suggested with a waggle of her eyebrows.

Kate gave a burst of laughter. "My better-than-a-boyfriend brownies? Trust me, I would give them up completely for the real deal."

Reaching across the table, Erin gripped her hand. "I know you would."

The understanding in her sister's voice brought an unexpected surge of emotion to Kate's chest and for a moment she struggled against the lump that formed in her throat. It wasn't that she missed Jack, because he had never made her feel they were true partners, but she was lonely and she was tired of pretending to be strong. What she wouldn't give to have a solid, caring man shoulder some of her burden. Someone like Holden.

"What about you?" she finally asked. "When's the last time you went on a date?"

Erin lifted one shoulder in a half-shrug. "I have high standards and I've yet to meet anyone who comes close to meeting them."

"Not even Griffin Jones?"

Erin's eyes shot to hers and her expression was cautious. "Why would you say that?"

"Because you work for him and because he's single and successful and very good-looking. I'd say he's the complete package."

Besides cooking at the diner, Erin was a certified public accountant and managed financial records and prepared tax returns for a small number of local clients, including the Bittersweet Brew Pub, owned by Griffin Jones and his two brothers. The clubby, nautical-themed restaurant and bar was a popular place to watch a sporting event or enjoy a hand-crafted beer.

"He's a client," Erin said flatly. "Did you miss the part where I said I have standards?"

"Okay, okay," Kate said, raising her hands in mock surrender. "Sorry. I didn't realize you were so sensitive about him."

"I'm not," Erin all but snapped. Then, seeing Kate's face, she gave a wry grin. "Okay, maybe I am, but it's only because he is the most aggravating man I've ever met. If it weren't for the fact he pays me very well—"

They were interrupted by the sound of an approaching vehicle. A pickup truck pulled into view beside the diner, oyster shells crunching beneath the tires. As she and Erin watched, Holden killed the engine and climbed out and began walking across the parking lot toward them. Kate's heart gave a leap and she devoured him with her eyes.

"And that's my cue to leave," Erin murmured.

"Oh, no, you don't have to go," Kate protested, knowing the words sounded weak and unconvincing.

But Erin only smiled and gave Kate a hug, lowering her voice and speaking into her ear. "Remember what I said. You need some fun in your life and I'm willing to bet he can provide it. I'll see you tomorrow." Releasing her, Erin walked past Holden with a cheerful greeting and made her way along the gravel road that led to the Belshaw house at the far end of the island.

Holden took the steps to the deck two at a time and approached Kate. He wore a pair of jeans and a black hooded sweatshirt. As he drew closer, she could see the beard growth that shadowed his jaw, as if he hadn't shaved in several days. He might have looked tough except for the warm expression in his coal-dark eyes.

"Hey, I got your message. And a missed call." He stepped closer. "I've been up near Eastport for the past few days and the reception was lousy. Your calls didn't drop into my phone until I was on my way home, near Bangor."

"Oh, that's okay," Kate said, assuming a casual tone she was far from feeling. Just seeing him again caused her heart to skip a crazy step-dance inside her chest. Of course he had a logical explanation for why he hadn't returned her calls. She should have known—she *had* known, but she'd let her imagination get carried away in thinking the worst. "I just wanted to thank you for the flowers. They were, uh, very special."

"I'm glad you like them."

"Did you choose those particular flowers yourself?" She knew the answer, but she had to ask.

"What?" He looked bemused for a moment. "No, sorry. The staff at the flower shop created the bouquet. Why? Is there something wrong with them?"

He was close enough now that she caught whiffs of the

unique scent she'd come to associate with him—a dry, woodsy fragrance with notes of ginger that made her want to inhale deeply. Without conscious thought, she moved nearer to him. "No, no, of course not, they're beautiful. It's just that flowers have meanings, and I wondered—never mind. If you didn't choose the blooms, it doesn't even matter."

"What meaning do the flowers have, Kate?" he asked, his eyes turning intent. She hadn't been aware of him moving, but there suddenly seemed to be no space between them. "Tell me, and then I'll tell you if the message they convey is true or not."

Kate swallowed hard. Why had she never noticed how thick and dark his eyelashes were? They drifted downward as his gaze fastened on her mouth, seemingly fascinated when she nervously moistened her lips.

"You'll think it's silly," she managed to say.

"Try me." Holden's voice was low and so compelling that Kate couldn't refuse him.

"There were pink camellias." Her voice sounded breathless and she could barely bring herself to meet his midnight gaze. "They symbolize longing."

One of his hands came up to caress the curve of her cheek. "At the risk of sounding like a tragic hero, true."

She could barely speak as his fingertips explored the under-side of her jaw and stroked along the sensitive skin of her throat. The sensation was electrifying, sending little bolts of pleasure zinging through her. She felt steeped in heat, from the crown of her head to the bottom of her heels. "White gardenias, which mean *You're lovely.*"

Another meaning behind the fragrant flower was *secret love*, but she didn't have the guts to tell him that.

"Also true," he murmured, as he cradled her cheek in his hand. His thumb caressed the heated ridge of her cheekbone. "You *are* lovely. What else?"

Kate swayed toward him and put a hand on his chest to steady herself. Beneath her palm, his heart worked in hard beats. "Purple heliotrope for devotion," she breathed, her gaze fixed on his mouth. Had she once thought it stern? Right now, all she could think was how perfect it had felt, molded to her own.

"I'm yours to command," he said, his voice a husky rasp, and then he lowered his head and covered her lips with his own.

Kate only distantly heard the needy sound that escaped her as he coaxed her mouth open and sank his tongue inside. His strong hand curled around the nape of her neck as he kissed her again and again, deep and unrestrained kisses, all urgent need and slick heat. Kate slid her arms around his neck as he kept kissing her, welcoming the rough demand of his mouth. *This.* This was what she wanted. This man and the intoxicating effect he had on her. She pushed her fingers into his hair, reveling in the texture of the heavy layers, and strained against his hard contours. She felt no shame, no embarrassment. Nothing had ever felt so delicious or right as this man kissing her, holding her, sliding one hand to the curve of her hip to press her subtly against the evidence of his arousal. Kate's body tightened, reminding her how good desire felt. It had been so long...

His kisses gentled, became softer, until finally he released her and drew her head to his shoulder. Panting, Kate pressed her fingers into the hard muscles of his back, reluctant to release him. He was warm and vital and he smelled incredible, an intoxicating blend of whatever soap or deodorant he used, combined with the unique scent that was his alone. She wanted to consume him. His hands rubbed soothing circles over her back and she felt his mouth press against her hair.

"Miss me?" he asked, his voice a seductive rumble in her ear.

"I didn't know you were headed out of town. You never said," she replied, lifting her face to look at him.

"It was unplanned," he replied. "A boat I've had my eye on suddenly became available, so my dad and I drove up to look at it."

"A lobster boat, you mean?"

Holden smiled, revealing the indent in his cheek. "Yes, a lobster boat."

"Did you buy her?"

"I put a deposit down, but I'm still waiting on the loan money to come through from the bank."

"So you will buy her," Kate clarified.

"I think so. She's new and she looks to be in great shape, better than the *Emily Ann*, and the price is too good to pass up."

"I can't wait to see her."

"You will." He released her and then hesitated, as if choosing his next words carefully. "When I dropped my dad off at his house, I saw Emily."

"Well, she does live there," Kate replied lightly, even as her heart gave an alarming lurch.

"She told me she and Sam had breakfast at the diner this morning and that you told them we were dating." He pushed his hands into the front pockets of his jeans as he watched her.

Kate cleared her throat. "I did, yes, but only because Emily *asked* if we were dating. I mean, we did go on a date, so technically that counts as dating. Doesn't it?"

Holden stared at her with a steady intensity. "That depends."

"On what?"

"On whether or not we're exclusive." His voice took on a deep, silken note. "I'd like us to be."

Kate felt winded, as if she couldn't quite catch her breath. She hadn't dated anyone seriously in the years since Jack's death. She was thirty-two years old and she'd only ever been with one guy. There was a part of her brain that argued she should get back out there and test the waters—date different people because her experience with the opposite sex was limited. But another part of her brain reasoned she didn't want a casual relationship.

"I just don't want to rush anything," she blurted, feeling suddenly anxious. "I want you to be sure."

He laughed softly and pulled her back into his arms. "Honey, I've never been more sure of anything in my life. Have dinner with me at my place tonight. Let me persuade you."

Before Kate could respond, there was the unmistakable growl of a car engine. They stepped apart just as a low, sleek Porsche pulled into view and parked beside Holden's pickup.

"Expecting someone?" Holden asked.

Kate watched in astonishment as the driver's door opened and Paul Bellecourt climbed out. Seeing her, he pulled off his sunglasses and grinned.

"Hello, darling. Surprised to see me?"

CHAPTER
ELEVEN

Holden watched, stunned, as the stocky, red-haired man closed the distance between them and bounded up the steps to the deck, arms open. Kate moved into them with a surprised laugh as he embraced her, air-kissing her on both cheeks.

"What are you doing here?" Kate asked, pulling back from him, even as he kept her hands firmly clasped in his own. "I mean, how did you even find me?"

Holden didn't need an introduction—he recognized the celebrity chef from the quick Google search he'd done on him after Kate had returned from New York City. His first thought was he appeared shorter in person, although he acknowledged most people looked short to him. He guessed Paul Bellecourt to be around forty. He was good-looking, with bright blue eyes and thick red hair that had a professionally tousled appearance. He oozed confidence and entitlement in the way only those with wealth and power could.

"I had to see this place for myself," he said to Kate. "You made it sound so charming, and you were right."

"Did you drive all the way here from New York?"

"I did," he confirmed, laughing. "All by myself, too. No camera crews or makeup artists in sight."

As if suddenly recalling Holden's presence, Kate turned toward him. "Paul, this is—" She faltered for a moment before rushing on. "This is Holden Foster. Holden, I'd like you to meet Paul Bellecourt. He taught the master class I attended in New York City."

Holden extended his hand. "Nice to meet you."

Paul gave his hand two strong pumps and Holden knew those shrewd blue eyes missed nothing, taking in his black hoodie, jeans and work boots and dismissing him as unimportant. "Good to meet you," he replied, and immediately turned back to Kate. "I'm staying at the Hummingbird Inn and Melanie Driscoll told me I might find you here." He made a show of admiring the iconic fifties-era diner and the flower-bedecked outside seating area. "What a gem! I can understand why you love living here."

"Yes, but why are you here?" Kate persisted. "Are you on vacation, or is there is something else that brings you all this way?"

"You, darling. You're the reason I've come all this way. Well, that and because it's Memorial Day weekend and I have a good friend who has a place a little north of here. But I came here specifically because I have a proposition for you." Paul shot Holden a glance. "If it's okay, I'd rather we spoke privately. Are you free for dinner tonight?"

"Well—" She looked helplessly at Holden, who raised both hands.

"It's fine, Kate."

"Oh!" Paul exclaimed in sudden understanding. "Do you already have plans?"

"No."

"No."

They both spoke at once, and Holden didn't miss the flush of color that rose in Kate's face, or the distress in her gray eyes.

"We don't have plans," he reassured her quietly, holding her gaze.

He recognized the significance of the celebrity chef coming all the way to Bittersweet Harbor, even if Kate did not. He realized now he'd been wrong when he'd believed Kate too provincial to attract Bellecourt. Whatever proposition the other man had in mind, Holden instinctively understood it was a ruse —an excuse—to get closer to her. He wished he could shake the sense of foreboding he felt, and silently cursed the other man for his poor timing. Just five more minutes and Kate would have agreed to have dinner with *him* that night, and Paul Bellecourt would have been out of luck. More importantly, Holden was certain she would have agreed to his suggestion of an exclusive relationship. Everything in him wanted to tell the other man to get back into his fancy car and leave Bittersweet Harbor. But he knew if he pressed Kate to go out with him instead of the chef, her heart wouldn't be in it. She'd be distracted and worried, and she'd spend the whole evening thinking about Paul Bellecourt and wondering why he was in Bittersweet Harbor and if she'd insulted him by refusing to go to dinner with him. No thanks. When he took Kate out again, she wouldn't be thinking about any other man.

"No, of course not," she murmured in response to his comment, and dragged her attention back to Paul. "What did you have in mind?"

"Some place quiet, where we can talk." He paused, and managed to look sheepish. "Melanie recommended Luigi's Restaurant, so I took the liberty of making reservations for six o'clock. I hope that's all right."

Kate flashed a glance at Holden, and he knew what she was thinking. Of all the places in town he could have chosen, why did it have to be there? "Yes, it's a lovely restaurant. I'll meet you there at six."

"Let me drive you," Paul coaxed. "I'll pick you up at five and you can give me a tour of the town before dinner."

"Oh!" Kate looked adorably distraught. "I'd love to, but I really can't get away until six o'clock. My son—"

"Say no more, I understand." To his credit, Bellecourt didn't press the issue. Instead, he gestured toward the diner. "I'd love to see the inside of your restaurant. Could you give me a quick peek now?"

Holden watched Kate carefully, noting the expressions that flitted across her face: surprise, reluctance, and then a bright smile that he recognized as being forced. Holden suspected any other woman would be in raptures to have Paul Bellecourt show up in her home town and express an interest in her life, but Kate wasn't like other women. She tended to shy away from attention. He also suspected his own presence made her feel awkward at being singled out by the famous pastry chef, never mind being alone with him. Holden didn't kid himself into thinking he was a big fan of the idea himself. He didn't want her alone with the guy and resented how the other man had not only shown up unannounced, but had gone ahead and made dinner reservations without knowing if Kate was free or if she even wanted to have dinner with him.

"Of course," she said now, smiling at Paul. "I was actually just locking up for the day, but if you'd like to take a look, I'll show you around."

Holden didn't miss how her eyes flicked to his as if in silent entreaty. There were all kinds of things he would have liked to say right then, but any of them would make him look and sound like a Neanderthal. He wished he could play the boyfriend card and throw his weight around a little, maybe insist on accompanying her to dinner with Bellecourt.

"Ah, there's my phone," he fibbed, pulling it out of his back pocket and pretending to look at the screen. "I'm just going to take this, if you don't mind."

He waited as Kate ushered Paul into the diner before leaning casually against the railing of the deck. He pretended to be absorbed in his phone, while keeping an ear tuned toward the open door. He could hear Kate's soft murmurings and Paul's deeper responses, although he couldn't make out their conversation. He straightened when they reappeared several minutes later and waited as Kate locked the diner.

"What a fantastic little place," Paul enthused. "If you ever want to part with any of the Elvis memorabilia, let me know. I can find you a very generous buyer."

"It's an amazing collection, but my family would never agree to sell anything," Kate said, giving him an apologetic look. "We did auction off a guitar last summer, but only because we needed the money to finance a new bridge across the Narrows. Otherwise, everything will eventually go to my son, Ryan."

"I understand," Paul said, smiling. "I hope I get the chance to meet your son while I'm here."

"How long are you planning to stay?" Holden asked.

Paul turned and looked at him as if surprised to see Holden still there. "I'm not sure," he replied. "As long as it takes, I suppose."

With that cryptic remark, he turned and made his way to his car. "I'll see you at six," he called to Kate.

Kate moved to stand beside Holden as Paul climbed into his sports car and with a cheery wave of his hand, drove away.

"What do you think he wants?" she asked.

"Oh, I know exactly what he wants," Holden replied grimly. "You."

HOLDEN TRIED and failed not to obsess about Kate's meeting with Paul Bellecourt. He refused to call it a date. But images of the two of them played out like an R-rated film in his head until he thought he would go nuts. He only barely restrained himself from doing a slow drive by the restaurant to see if he could glimpse them through the windows; he even had his truck keys in his hand before he realized how insane he would appear if— God forbid—Kate were to spot him. She'd think he was a total stalker. He'd never felt so impotent. Instead, he grabbed a cold beer from his fridge and retreated to his workshop, where he turned up the music and buried himself in his latest wood-working project, a set of four Adirondack chairs and two small side tables. The process of measuring and cutting the wood, along with the high-pitched whine of power tools and the distinctive gingery fragrance of the freshly cut Port-Orford cedar, never failed to calm him.

He told himself Kate was too smart to fall for the celebrity chef, no matter how lavishly he wined and dined her. Aside from the master class, she barely knew the guy. But as he used a hand planer on a length of cedar, he recalled again Bellecourt's brash confidence and winning smile. There was no question the guy had charisma in spades and he wouldn't blame Kate if she found herself falling for his charm. After all, she'd fallen for Jack and his shallow attention. But he'd be damned if he'd let her go without a fight this time. He'd lost her once before. He wouldn't do it again. He wasn't an insecure eighteen-year-old anymore. He'd tell her how he felt, how he'd always felt. Then, if she told him she didn't feel the same way and could never see herself with him, he'd let her go. But the thought of her with Bellecourt made him want to put a fist through something.

He painstakingly cut and assembled two chairs on his workbench before setting them aside. Outside, the sky was dark and glancing at his watch he realized he'd been at it for more than three hours. It was nearly nine o'clock. Where was Kate now? Had she gone home after dinner, or had Bellecourt persuaded her to continue their evening together, maybe get a nightcap somewhere? He was certain Kate wouldn't go back to the Hummingbird Inn with him—they were one of her biggest clients and she knew everyone who worked there. In fact, if he knew her the way he thought he did, she'd probably begged off right after dinner and was at home, baking. She also had Ryan to consider. At fourteen, he was old enough to stay by himself but Holden knew Kate preferred to be home in the evenings to make sure he had dinner, did his homework, and didn't stay up too late.

Turning down the music, Holden walked over to the open doorway of the workshop and looked across the marshes and saltwater estuaries to where the lights of Bittersweet Harbor twinkled in the distance. The Nanick Lighthouse blinked steadily, guarding the entrance to the mouth of the river. He could hear the crash of the surf in the distance and the cool night air carried the salty scent of the sea and the marshes. He should pack it in and head to bed since he needed to be up again in less in than six hours, but he felt restless and frustrated, unable to dispel a sense of impending doom.

Had he spent the past five years fooling himself, believing Kate would one day wake up and realize it was him she belonged with? Bellecourt's unexpected arrival in Bittersweet Harbor had all his alarm bells going off and his old insecurities struggled to the surface. Maybe the only reason Kate was still single was because she hadn't found anyone appealing enough to commit herself to—including himself. Even the memory of their shared kiss wasn't enough to reassure him. She could be playing with him until someone better came along. In the next instant he knew that wasn't true. Kate would never be less than authentic. She wouldn't play games. That wasn't her style. He hated that he felt so unsure of himself, but for him the stakes had never been higher.

Returning to his workbench, he swept the wood shavings from the table and floor and put away his tools. He switched off the music and the overhead light before stepping outside to pull the sliding barn door closed. He was walking toward the house when his phone vibrated in his pocket. Pulling it out, he saw Kate's name on the display.

"Kate," he answered, feeling equal amounts of relief and anxiety. "Everything okay?"

"Yes. I just wanted to let you know I'm home."

"Okay." He paused. "How did it go tonight?"

He braced himself for whatever Kate might say. He'd come up with a million different reasons for why Bellecourt had wanted her to have dinner with him and what the mysterious proposal might entail, none of them good.

"Well, it was a little overwhelming, to be honest," she replied. "But I don't want to talk about it over the phone. Can I see you?"

"Now? Tonight?"

She must have heard the surprise in his voice because she immediately apologized. "I'm sorry, forget it. I know it's late."

"No, no, it's fine," he reassured her. "I was just finishing up some work in the barn. Let me come over there."

"I can drive out to your place."

"No, I'll come to you," he said firmly.

"Okay." He heard the relief in her voice. "I'll see you soon."

She was sitting on her front steps when he pulled up in front of her town house less than ten minutes later. The lamps on either side of the front door cast a soft light over her. As soon as she saw his truck she stood and walked to the gate. She wore a short, blue floral dress that floated around her thighs and had wrapped herself in a soft shawl. As he parked, she opened the gate and approached the truck. Leaning across the seat, he opened the passenger door for her.

"Get in," he said. "It's too cold to sit outside."

He waited until she had climbed in and closed the door before he adjusted the heat vents to give her more warmth.

"Thanks for coming so quickly," she murmured. "I didn't know who else to call."

Holden didn't point out that she had a mother and four sisters, not to mention numerous close girlfriends in town, any of whom would have dropped everything to be with her. He was just glad it had been him and some of his apprehension eased.

"You can always call me," he said. "Any time, night or day. Now tell me what's going on."

He shifted sideways in his seat and watched as she plucked at the soft shawl, not meeting his eyes. After a moment she blew out a hard breath.

"Paul wants me to run a new bakery he's opening soon." She gave a helpless shrug. "It's the opportunity of a lifetime."

"And yet, you don't sound excited."

She raised her head. Her gaze clung to his. "Because it would mean relocating to Cambridge, Massachusetts."

Holden felt his eyebrows go up and he blew out a hard breath. He felt as if someone had socked him hard in the gut. "Wow."

"Yeah," she said with a weak smile. "Wow."

In that instant, Holden wanted to tell her all the reasons why she shouldn't consider the offer, including his own feelings for her. He wanted to tell her that Paul was dangling this carrot as an excuse to get close to her, not because he needed someone for his bakery. A guy like that could have the best of the best. There was only one reason why he'd asked Kate to come work for him and it had nothing to do with her baking skills. But he knew how dismissive and cruel those words would sound, so he remained silent. This was her decision to make and he instinctively knew anything he said to persuade her to stay might have the opposite effect.

"Tell me what he said," he urged, instead.

"He bought a bakery in Harvard Square about six months ago and has been renovating it. The grand opening is in three months and he wants me to come work for him as the lead baker."

She didn't need to explain to Holden what this might mean for her dream of one day owning her own bakery. To work for Paul Bellecourt—to have him as her mentor and boss—would open all kinds of doors for her. Under any other circumstances, Holden would be elated for her and encourage her to go for it, but he strongly suspected Bellecourt was looking for more than just a lead baker.

"What about Ryan?" he asked.

"He'd stay here, at least initially." Kate flicked a glance at Holden and then looked out the window toward her small, brick townhouse. "Paul wants to send me to a three-month culinary school in New York with an eye toward becoming a head pastry chef one day. He thinks my skills are wasted here in Bittersweet Harbor."

Holden frowned. "And he would pay for it, I suppose?"

"Well, yes. He said it would be an investment, since I'd work for him and learn everything there is to know about being a pastry chef. He offered a very competitive salary."

"I'm sure he did," Holden muttered. "But where would you live, Kate? Cambridge isn't exactly affordable, and it's definitely not within commuting distance." An affluent suburb of Boston, the elite enclave boasted Harvard University and MIT, and Holden knew the cost of living in Cambridge exceeded that of Boston.

"Well that's just it," she replied, turning to look at him with cautious eyes. "Paul has a condo in Cambridge that he almost never uses. He said Ryan and I could live there for as long as we need to. We'd pay rent, of course. Ryan could go to school there and Paul said he could even join the local sailing club. Apparently, they sail every day on the Charles River. You know how much he would love that."

Holden scoffed softly. The bastard had thought of everything. How could Kate not see Bellecourt's true motive? Holden wanted to shake her, or kiss her until she forgot she'd ever heard the name Paul Bellecourt.

"You said you didn't like the city," he reminded her.

"Yes, but that was New York City, this is Cambridge. It's not as big and it's a college town. Ryan could really thrive there."

He pinioned her with a hard look. "So this is about Ryan?"

"Well, no, it's—it's about both of us. It's about giving Ryan the best chance to succeed, and it's about my career," she stammered. "I'll never have this kind of opportunity again."

"When do you need to decide?"

"Paul is driving up to Seal Harbor tomorrow for a weekend get-together at Martha Stewart's summer home. He's coming back here on Sunday night and wants me drive down to Boston with him on Monday. He said he needs for me to decide soon."

Holden stared at her for a long moment. "Monday is Memorial Day. You're going to miss your family's barbeque?"

"I'm sure they can do without me for one day. As long as I send Ryan and some desserts, they'll be happy." She paused, looking at him with wide, worried eyes. "Am I doing the right thing?"

"I can't make this decision for you, Kate, but I will say one thing: I don't want you to go. I understand how big this chance is and what it could mean for you, but I don't want you to leave. I can't see you being happy in Cambridge."

"Holden—"

"Everyone you love—everyone who loves you—is here, in Bittersweet Harbor. Ryan's friends are here, his grandparents, too."

I'm here.

"I know, and that's what I've been struggling with. Do I have the right to uproot him from everything he loves? But Cambridge is only a few hours away, we could come back anytime we want." She paused, her expression pleading for him to understand. "This is more than I'd ever dreamed was possible, Holden."

He nodded, not looking at her. "I know. I just wonder if you're chasing your dream, or helping Bellecourt chase his?"

"What do you mean?"

"Forget it," he said, and dragged his hand through his hair. "All I'm saying is be careful. He wants to own you, Kate, and if you're living in his condo and working in his bakery and getting paid from his pocket, then he will own you. One way or another, he'll own you. Is that what you want?"

She frowned. "You're wrong. He only wants to help me." She lifted her chin. "He thinks I have real potential."

"Kate," he said, striving for patience. "He wants *you*."

"You keep saying that, but you're wrong. He's done nothing but behave like a perfect gentleman." Her tone had turned peevish, defensive.

"Trust me, honey," Holden said quietly. "I'm a man. I see right through him."

Her gray eyes turned cool. "Are you saying he wasn't being truthful when he told me I had potential?"

"*No.* Of course not. You're smart and creative and you have more potential than anyone I know. But that's not the reason he wants you to come to Boston. He's doing everything he can to get you away from here because once you're there, you'll be alone. You'll need to rely upon him for everything."

"No. That's not true," she said softly, but Holden didn't miss the sudden doubt in her eyes. "I'm going to look at the bakery and the condo with him on Monday, and then I'll decide."

"Let me come with you."

But she was already reaching for the door handle. "No, thank you. I'll be fine."

"*Kate.*" She paused to look at him. "How will you get there and back? At least let me drive you."

"Thanks, but I'll drive down with Paul and catch a train back to Portland. Just let me do this, Holden. I don't know yet if I'll take him up on his offer, but I need to at least consider it."

With a low growl, Holden caught her by the arm and turned her fully toward him. "Then consider this when you're making your decision," he muttered and leaning across the seat, he imprisoned her face between his hands and covered her mouth with his. The kiss wasn't gentle; it was forceful and demanding, infused with all the pent-up need and frustration he'd been holding inside since Bellecourt's appearance—since he was eighteen, if he was being honest.

Kate resisted, pushing one hand against his chest. With a sound of impatience, Holden pressed her back against the seat and deepened the kiss, sweeping his tongue against hers as he invaded the hot, satiny recesses of her mouth. He wanted to consume her, to take her there in the front seat of his truck. He wanted to imprint himself upon her so there would be doubt about who she belonged with. He knew the exact instant when she yielded, softening beneath him even as her hand lifted from his chest and crept up to cradle his jaw. She made an inarticulate sound of surrender and then she was kissing him back, winding her arms around his neck and straining toward him across the center console. Holden groaned and gathered her closer, spearing his tongue against hers in lush, erotic sweeps. He flicked her shawl open and slid his hand over her breast. She gasped into his mouth and arched against his palm. Holden ached to haul her across the seat and onto his lap. Dragging his mouth from hers, he turned his face into her neck, inhaling her scent as he smoothed a hand over her hair.

"You drive me crazy," he muttered, nuzzling against her skin. "Let me love you, Kate. Come back to my house. Now, tonight."

Kate's breath came in soft pants against his cheek and her hands pushed weakly at his shoulders. "Holden, wait. No, stop. *Please.*"

Holden lifted his head and searched her eyes. Some of the haze of arousal lifted when he saw the distress in her eyes. "What is it?" He cupped her cheek and stroked his thumb over her cheekbone. "Do I scare you?"

"No," she said. "But this is moving too fast. I need some time, and I can't think straight when I'm with you. I can't even breathe."

Holden gave a soft huff of laughter, because that had been his reality for the past fifteen years, whenever he was with her. She'd had him tangled in knots for years and she still didn't realize her effect on him. She had no idea about the power she had over him, or that everything he did was with her in mind.

"I can fix that," he promised, his voice low and roughened by emotion. "Come home with me now, or invite me in."

For just an instant he saw the longing in her eyes, but she withdrew from his hold and reached for the edges of her wrap, pulling it around herself like a shield. Her eyes were silvered by the light from the nearby street lamp, and her lips looked bee-stung from his kisses. Holden wanted to reach for her again, but he could actually see her withdrawing from him, both physically and emotionally, and he wanted to howl with frustration.

"I'm sorry but I can't, Holden." Her voice was unsteady. "I need some space, and I need time to think."

Holden tamped down his rising aggravation and reluctantly released her and eased back in his seat. "Don't go with him, Kate. Stay here. Whatever it is you think he can give you isn't worth what you'd be giving up."

She pushed her hair back with one hand and stared. "Which is...what?"

"Us."

CHAPTER
TWELVE

S leep eluded Kate that night. She lay alone in the small front bedroom and watched the shadows on the wall and replayed the astounding—and alarming—events of the evening. Could two men be any more different? Not only in looks, but in temperament. Paul had been good-humored and effusive during dinner at Luigi's, ordering the most expensive items on the menu and regaling her with amusing anecdotes, all while complimenting her on the smallest things, from her hair and her smile, to the dessert she'd finally selected at his insistence. He'd made her feel special, as if he couldn't do enough for her—opening doors and holding chairs and waiting expectantly as she sampled each morsel of food, as if he'd prepared each item himself. Kate hadn't been unaware of the attention they'd drawn from the other diners, and the owner of the restaurant had only made it worse by coming to their table to personally inquire how they were enjoying their meal.

When Paul had finally told her he wanted her to manage his new bakery, she had been speechless. Her initial response had been to adamantly refuse—she knew nothing about managing a high-end pastry shop—but Paul had been unrelenting in his persuasiveness. He'd had a compelling counter-argument for every one of her objections until finally, exhausted by his persistence, she had agreed to go to Boston with him on Monday to see the bakery, as well as the condo he'd insisted was hers to use. She wouldn't accept the condo offer, of course. If she decided to do this, she would find her own place to live.

Could Holden be right? Did Paul expect more from her than he'd let on? Suddenly, all the innocent touches and smiles he'd given her took on new significance. She didn't want to believe he'd made the offer for any reason other than he'd recognized her talent as a baker, but what did she know? The only relationship she'd ever had had been with Jack and now, to a lesser extent, Holden, who'd made no pretense about what *he* wanted from her. The knowledge both thrilled and alarmed her.

Rolling over in bed, she bunched her pillow beneath her cheek as images of Holden crushed any further thoughts of Paul Bellecourt. He'd told her she drove him crazy. He'd wanted her to go home with him, right then and there. If not for the fact her son was asleep in the townhouse, she might have gone with him. She recalled again the heat and power of his body as he'd kissed her in the front seat of his truck, dragging long-dormant sensations to the surface. Every time he touched her, flames sparked to life. A small part of her acknowledged that if they hadn't been parked in front of her house and if the center console hadn't impeded them, she might have let him do whatever he wanted. *What she wanted.* Just the memory of the sensual intent in his dark eyes caused heat to course through her body and she pushed the covers aside, desperate for the cool night air on her skin. Instead, all she felt was Holden's hands on her.

She didn't know what to do. Holden had all but begged her not to go to Boston with Paul, but she couldn't refuse what Paul was offering without at least knowing what that was. She needed to see the bakery and get a sense of what her life might be like if she did choose to accept his offer. She'd put her dreams on hold once before when she'd left college to become a wife and mother. She wouldn't do it again.

Groaning in frustration, she reached for her phone to check the time. It was barely three o'clock in the morning. With a defeated sigh she sat up and scrubbed her hands over her face. Her unexpected dinner plans with Paul had meant she hadn't done any baking for her morning deliveries. She always kept some frozen pastries and baked goods in reserve for just these situations but decided since she couldn't sleep, she might as well bake.

She peeked in at Ryan as she passed his room. He lay on his stomach, mouth open as he slept, looking impossibly young. His blankets had slid almost to the floor, so she tiptoed in and covered him before she carefully closed his door and made her way downstairs to the kitchen. She put her earbuds in, selected a playlist from her phone and began pulling ingredients out of the pantry. Soon she was too absorbed in the process of measuring and mixing to be distracted by thoughts of Holden Foster and his potent kisses. When the alarm on her phone finally rang, she realized it was six o'clock and she'd been at it for nearly three hours. She would have just enough time to wake Ryan, load her baked goods into the van and make her morning deliveries before she needed to be at the diner. And maybe, if she was lucky, the day would bring a clearer vision of what her future might hold.

∽

HER LAST DELIVERY that morning was to the Hummingbird Inn, a gorgeous old Victorian home that had been lovingly restored and turned into a charming bed and breakfast. As Kate pulled into the small parking lot beside the sprawling house, she wished she'd put the inn first on her list of deliveries, when most of the guests would be guaranteed to still be sleeping. What if she ran into Paul? He was staying here, after all. She reminded herself she was only bringing the bins of pastries into the kitchen. Celebrity chef or not, he wouldn't dare impose on the kitchen staff at this early hour—would he? She wasn't prepared to see him, not yet. Not with Holden's warnings still ringing in her ears.

With her arms full, she managed to open the door that led to the kitchen and sidle in sideways. She found herself in a small utility room where she paused, straining to hear any evidence that Paul might be in the adjoining kitchen. Satisfied the coast was clear, she carried the bins through and set them down on a stainless steel work surface.

Melanie Driscoll, whose family owned the inn, turned from where she was filling a crystal pitcher with orange juice and smiled at her. An attractive woman in her late forties, she managed the day to day operation of the inn. "Oh, there you are. Right on time, as always."

"Yes, but I can't stay," Kate said as she opened the first bin and began pulling out trays of assorted muffins.

"Oh, my goodness," Melanie exclaimed as she breathed deeply. "I can smell those from over here. Did you bake those this morning?"

"I did, actually."

Melanie set the pitcher of juice down on the work surface next to a second pitcher of tomato juice and helped Kate remove the breakfast pastries from the containers and then arranged them on a pretty, flowered serving platter. "They look and smell amazing. I have some guests who are early risers, so I'll just bring these out to the breakfast room." She pinioned Kate with a stern look. "Don't you dare leave until I return—I have a million questions for you."

"Melanie, I really can't stay—"

"Five minutes, that's all." She deftly picked up both pitchers and the platter of muffins and swept out of the kitchen before Kate could protest further.

With a resigned sigh, Kate emptied the bins, placing blueberry, cranberry-orange, and banana-nut muffins on a large tray alongside her homemade breakfast Danishes. She was stacking the empty bins inside one another when Melanie returned.

"Is it true?" the older woman asked without preamble. "Are you going to work for Paul Bellecourt? I nearly died when he booked a room here and then when he showed up, the first thing he asked was where he could find you! He's shorter than he looks on his cooking shows," she mused, before rushing on, barely pausing to take a breath. "I know you attended his master baking class, but you must have really made an impression for him to come all the way up here."

"Oh, well, he didn't come up here just to see me—"

"I overheard him say he's spending the weekend at Martha Stewart's summer house," Melanie exclaimed. "Oh, to have that kind of life. Please tell me you're going to work for him. Just imagine—you could have a home in the Hamptons one day, or even live next door to Martha herself!"

"I'm not sure about that. He's looking for someone to manage his newest bakery, but nothing's been decided yet," Kate said evasively.

"Well, of course you're going to accept. Why wouldn't you? It's the opportunity of a lifetime, Kate. Can you really see yourself staying here and baking muffins and desserts for the local restaurants when you could be part of Paul Bellecourt's food empire?"

"It would mean moving to the Boston area."

"So?"

Kate gave the older woman a tolerant look. "I'm not sure I want to be that far away from my family."

"Pssht. Boston isn't that far. You could be back and forth in a day." Seeing Kate's doubt, she put a hand on her arm. "This is Paul Bellecourt, Kate. If nothing else, work for him for a year or two and then branch out on your own. You've been saying you want to start your own business and what better way than by running one of his bakeries?" She gave Kate a benevolent smile. "I wouldn't be at all surprised if, in a few years, you started your own baking business and gave him a run for his money."

Kate laughed. "Well, I'm not sure that's true, but I appreciate your faith in me." She shrugged. "There's just a lot to consider and I'm not sure now is the right time."

Melanie's expression turned knowing. "Does your reluctance to leave Bittersweet Harbor have anything to do with a certain hunky lobsterman?"

"Why would you think that?" she asked, even as she felt a telltale blush heat her face.

"Oh, a little birdie told me you and Holden Foster have been seeing each other. Don't get me wrong, I think it's great—they don't come any better than him."

"I didn't realize you knew Holden."

"He's friends with my nephew, Tyler Goodwin. You must know him, since you went to school together."

Kate recalled a guy whose physique looked as if it had been hewn from the local granite, and a nose that had been badly broken at some point. He'd helped to rebuild the new bridge that linked Scanty Island to the mainland. "If it's the same guy I'm thinking of, he graduated a few years behind me so we didn't really know each other. He works for Englebright Engineering, right?"

"He does now, but he and Holden became friends years ago when they both worked at one of the marinas," Melanie confirmed.

"I do remember him." Kate pointed vaguely toward her own nose. "He broke his..."

"Oh, yes." Melanie rolled her eyes. "An accident at the boat yard and he was too stubborn to see a doctor, which is why it was never fixed. Still, I don't think it detracts from his looks. I've always thought a man shouldn't be too pretty. Holden broke his own nose around the same time if I remember correctly, but of course you know all about that."

In fact, Kate had no idea how Holden had broken his nose, only that it had happened while she'd been away at college. She'd asked Jack about it once and he'd looked askance at her.

"Why are you asking me?" he'd demanded, his eyes narrowed with suspicion.

"Because he's your friend?" she'd ventured. "I was just curious."

"Then ask him," he'd retorted.

Kate hadn't brought the subject up again. Now she found herself wondering just how it had happened. "What's the story you heard?" she asked casually. "I'll tell you if it's true or not."

Melanie busied herself stacking the remaining pastries onto a tray and arranging the muffins in a pretty basket. "The way I heard it, Jack broke it when he and Holden got into a brawl." Looking up, she saw Kate's expression. "Wait—you really didn't know? Well, don't let it upset you. They were young. Boys get into fights even when they're friends. The good news is they got past it and didn't let it ruin their friendship." She smiled. "And that broken beak didn't do Holden any harm, either. Makes him look a little dangerous, if you know what I mean."

But Kate barely heard her. Her mind spun as she tried to recall the details of the single semester she'd spent at college.

Holden had driven up to Orono to drop off a dorm-sized refrigerator for her and his nose most definitely had not been broken then. He'd sensed something was wrong and had pressed her until she'd told him about the pregnancy and how Jack wasn't returning her calls, before she'd promptly dissolved into tears and had cried in his arms like a baby. He'd left soon after, his jaw tight and his eyes hard. She'd always thought he'd been upset with her, but he'd recently assured her that hadn't been the case at all. She hadn't seen Holden again until the wedding. She'd been vaguely aware of him standing at the back of the church looking big and grim. Not only had his nose been broken, but both eyes had still been bruised. He hadn't stayed for the small reception in the basement of the church afterwards, and she had soon forgotten all about it. Now, a niggling suspicion began to take shape in her head.

"I'm sorry, but I have to go or I'm going to be late for work," she said, forcing a smile. "I'll let you know what happens with the bakery."

"Please do," Melanie said. "And I'll be sure to tell Mr. Bellecourt where his breakfast pastries came from this morning."

Kate stashed the empty bins in the back of her van and was opening the driver's door when someone called her name. Turning, she saw Paul Bellecourt walking toward her from the kitchen. Dressed in a pair of loose jeans and a pastel blue button-down shirt that complemented his coloring, he came quickly around the back of the van.

"I'm glad I caught you," he said, smiling. He indicated the blueberry muffin in his hand. "Delicious, by the way. I brought it with me because I didn't want to risk the wait staff throwing it away while I was out here."

Kate smiled. "I'm sure your breakfast was safe. Did you sleep well?"

"I did, yeah. The rooms here are very comfortable, but I was up at the crack of dawn. I took a jog along the boardwalk and through town. I was surprised how many restaurants and pubs you have here."

"More every year, it seems. The town attracts a lot of summer tourists."

"I can understand why," Paul said. "It's an absolutely lovely little town. Anyway, I'm glad I caught you. I'm heading up to Seal Harbor this morning but I'll be back to pick you up on Monday, say around ten o'clock? That should put us in Boston around lunch time. That is, if you're still interested."

"I am," Kate assured him. "More than ever, actually. I'll be ready to go at ten o'clock."

"Are you sure I can't persuade you to spend the night in the city?" He raised both hands. "No funny business. I'd love to show you some of my favorite places and there's a spectacular little breakfast joint in Arlington I think you'd love."

"No, I can't—I'm working on Tuesday and with the holiday weekend, it would be hard for me to find a replacement."

"Think about it," he urged.

"I will." She climbed into the van. "Have fun in Seal Harbor. I'll see you on Monday."

Paul lifted his hand in farewell as she drove out of the parking lot and through town, quiet at this hour except for the delivery trucks. She took a detour through the marina where Holden kept his boat. Her heart pounded hard at the prospect of confronting him with her suspicions. But while his truck was parked in the lot, the *Emily Ann* was nowhere to be seen. By then she'd had a chance to reconsider her actions and was relieved to have missed him. What would she have said to him, anyway? That she knew Jack had busted his nose fifteen years ago?

She sat for a moment in the marina parking lot and stared blindly at the water as memories washed over her. When

Holden had visited her at college, Jack had been in Texas. So if the two of them really had gotten into a brawl, either Jack had been back in Bittersweet Harbor without her knowledge, or Holden had flown to Texas to confront him. She gave a soft huff of bitter laughter, because all the pieces were beginning to slide into place. She could see it so clearly in her mind's eye; Holden insisting that Jack do the right thing by her, and Jack telling Holden to go to hell. But even if they'd fought, there was no way Jack would have married her unless he'd actually wanted to. Even Holden couldn't have forced him to do something so drastic against his will—could he?

With an agonized groan, Kate scrubbed her hands over her face and then dragged in several deep breaths. Did any of it even matter anymore? Jack *had* married her. He'd left school and had come back to Bittersweet Harbor and had married her in a small, private ceremony. The marriage had been far from perfect, but Jack had loved her and Ryan. Even as she thought it, a small voice whispered that she was a liar. Jack had never wanted to marry her. He'd joined the army almost immediately after Ryan's birth. He'd deliberately chosen to face a lethal enemy on the other side of the world rather than spend any time with her and the baby. She'd loved him, but he had never loved her. Not really. He'd cared about her, but he'd never been in love with her. She'd tried so hard to make him happy, to be what he wanted, never knowing what she was doing wrong or why he didn't love her.

She'd failed him.

She thought she'd come to terms with that truth years ago, but the knowledge still had the ability to hurt her and she angrily swiped at her damp cheeks.

She didn't want to shed any more tears for Jack Prescott. She'd already wasted too many on him. But if what she suspected was true, neither could she forgive Holden for his interference all those years ago. She'd often thought what her life might have been like if she and Jack hadn't gotten married. She could have stayed in school, maybe put Ryan into a daycare center on campus while she attended classes. The university had financial aid programs specifically designed for students who were single parents. Instead, she'd married Jack and they'd both been miserable. She didn't know exactly what Holden had done to make Jack marry her, but he should never have interfered. He might have changed the course of her life once, but she wouldn't let him do it again.

THIRTEEN

Holden knew he needed to back off and give Kate some space, but the primitive part of his brain wanted to drag her back to his house and lay claim to her in true caveman fashion. Instead, he threw himself into his work. He'd spent Friday on his lobster boat, hauling traps and dropping new ones and when he finally got home, he forced himself to finish the set of Adirondack chairs he'd been working on, before he repaired the dozen or so traps he had stacked beside the barn. The physical work made him tired, but it didn't stop his mind from working overtime.

The bank had finally come through with the money he needed to buy the second lobster boat and while he should have been elated, all he could think about was Kate and the expression on her face when she'd left him. He'd basically given her an ultimatum: him or Bellecourt. He regretted his impulsive words because he knew it didn't matter if she went to Boston or stayed in Bittersweet Harbor—he would do whatever it took to make their relationship work, even if it meant driving to Cambridge to see her. He'd been an idiot for backing her into a corner and for all he knew, his arrogant posturing might have driven her away.

By Saturday afternoon he'd decided he couldn't stand by for another second without talking to her, but his calls went to voicemail and she didn't respond to his texts. He felt impotent, angry and frustrated. Only the miniscule amount of pride he had left prevented him from driving over to her house and banging on her door, insisting she speak to him. Instead, he called his father. He needed to get away before he did something epically stupid, like tracking her down and declaring his undying love for her. He would never manipulate her that way. If she was going to stay in Bittersweet Harbor, let it be because she wanted to and not because he'd emotionally blackmailed her into doing so.

"Hey, Dad," he said, when Ethan Foster answered the phone. "The bank came through with the money for the boat and I wondered if you'd head back to Eastport with me and help me bring her home."

"When would you want to leave?"

"Today, if possible. We can spend tonight in Eastport and head back tomorrow."

"We need to come home so soon?" his father asked, amusement lacing his voice. "There's a little too much estrogen in the house right now with your sister and her friend here. I could use an escape."

His words pulled a reluctant laugh out of Holden. "Then throw an overnight bag together and I'll see you in an hour."

He called the owner of the boat to let him know he was coming up to collect the boat and then packed his own overnight bag. He stopped at the bank to obtain a draft for the amount he still owed, and then drove to where his parents lived on the edge of town. His mother, Laura, was standing at the kitchen stove when he let himself in through the back door, and the air was filled with the tantalizing aroma of homemade marinara sauce.

"Hey, Mom," he said, pressing a kiss to her cheek. "Spaghetti and meatballs for dinner tonight?"

"Hi, honey," she said, smiling at him. "That was the plan until you decided to abscond for the weekend with your father. Both Emily and Sam are working late tonight so I suppose this can wait until tomorrow night, although I had planned to do barbeque ribs. Will you join us for dinner tomorrow night?"

Holden hesitated. "Are the girls going to be here?"

"I'm assuming they will, why?"

"If you don't mind, I'll pass."

His mother laughed softly as she continued to stir the rich sauce. "I understand. Do you have plans with Kate Prescott?" She cast him a knowing look. "I hear the two of you are dating."

Holden blew out a breath. "I'm not sure we are, to be honest. She's been offered an opportunity to work for Paul Bellecourt in Cambridge, Mass."

His mother's dark eyes were gentle as she considered him. "You've liked her for a long time. Surely that's not a deal breaker for you, is it? Cambridge isn't *that* far, and you're willing to drive four hours to see a boat."

Holden suppressed a smile. Leave it to his mother to put things into perspective. "It's not a deal breaker for me," he admitted. "But I don't trust Bellecourt. I think he has another reason for asking Kate to move to Cambridge. I don't think he's being honest with her." He paused. "I also may have implied that if she takes the job, she'll lose any chance she might otherwise have had with me."

"Oh, Holden, you didn't!" his mother admonished, looking at him with a mixture of dismay and concern.

"Didn't what?" They both turned to see Holden's father

enter the kitchen, a small duffel bag in one hand. "What did I miss?"

"Kate Prescott is thinking of relocating to Cambridge," his mother said mournfully.

Ethan fixed Holden with an inscrutable look. "I'm going to miss her blueberry muffins."

His mother rolled her eyes at him and turned back to the stove with a muttered, "*Men.*"

"When does she leave?" Ethan asked.

"She's going to Cambridge on Monday to look at the bakery Paul Bellecourt wants her to manage, and he also offered her the use of a condo he owns there," Holden replied, his tone reflecting his displeasure. "If she accepts, he intends to send her to a twelve-week culinary school in New York before she begins working for him."

"My," Laura exclaimed, her eyebrows shooting upward. "She really made an impression on him."

"What are you going to do?" his father asked.

"What can I do?" Holden couldn't keep the bitterness out of his voice.

"Well, you're not a teenager anymore. Maybe start by telling her how you feel." His mother cast him a sideward look. "Just be honest with her."

"At least then you'll know where you stand," his father added.

Holden knew they were right, but the thought of laying his heart bare and becoming that vulnerable scared him more than he cared to admit. What if she didn't feel the same way? Worse, what if she rejected him and didn't want to see him again? At least during the past five years, he'd been able to see her and spend time with her, even if she had no idea about his feelings for her. Telling her how he felt could ruin everything.

"One thing you've never been is a coward," Ethan Foster said, his voice low. "If you want this girl, then fight for her."

Holden knew his father was right. He hadn't put up any kind of fight for Kate in high school. Instead, he'd allowed Jack to swoop in and seduce her away with his charm and good looks. Hell, even when Jack had finally revealed his true colors, Holden hadn't taken advantage of the situation. Instead, he'd all but forced Jack to marry Kate. His only defense was he'd wanted Kate to be happy and he'd naively believed marriage to Jack was the answer.

Now he just hoped Paul Bellecourt's fancy French bakery and expensive Cambridge condo wouldn't sway her toward the other man. Holden recognized the opportunity Bellecourt offered was almost too good to pass up, but would Kate fall for Paul? The professional pastry chef was both charming and persuasive and could give Kate things that Holden never could. How could he compete with that? He'd never been any good with words or feelings, but grimly acknowledged they were all he had.

"I'll talk to her as soon as we get back," he promised. He'd tell her how he felt before she left for Cambridge. Whatever happened after that, at least he'd know he'd done his best.

"WHAT ARE you going to call her?" Ethan asked the following afternoon, after they had unhitched the forty-two foot lobster boat at the marina where Holden kept the *Emily Ann*.

"I haven't decided yet," Holden said as they stood in the parking lot and admired the vessel. With a navy blue hull and bright white topside and cabin, she almost sparkled. He tried and failed to prevent his gaze from drifting across the harbor to

KAREN FOLEY

the All Shook Up Diner, where he knew Kate must be getting ready to go home following the busy Sunday lunch shift.

"She's a beauty, but she could be a handful. How many crew are you going to bring on board?"

Pulling his attention back to the lobster boat, Holden rubbed a hand across the back of his neck. He and Tuck were easily able to captain and crew the smaller *Emily Ann*, but he'd likely need an additional man to work the new vessel.

"I'll bring on a sternman and a third man," he replied. "I heard Sully's oldest son is looking for work and he has experience."

"How much will Tuck pay you for captaining the *Emily Ann*?"

Holden gave his father a meaningful look. "He'll pay the going rate. If this boat works out the way I hope it will, maybe I'll let Tuck buy the *Emily Ann*."

His father clapped him on the shoulder. "Sounds like a plan, son. Never have more boats than you can pilot yourself."

"If you weren't so set on retirement, I'd ask you to captain the *Emily Ann*. Your fishing license is still good, isn't it?"

But Ethan just laughed. "Thanks, but no thanks, son. My days of getting up at dawn are over and my back can't handle pulling those traps."

At sixty-five, Ethan was still a robust man but Holden didn't begrudge his father his retirement. He'd worked as a lobsterman for nearly fifty years and he deserved to spend his current years just enjoying life. Before Holden could say as much, a minivan turned into the parking lot and drew to a stop alongside his pickup truck.

Kate.

Holden's heart leapt.

"And that's my cue to leave," Ethan murmured.

"Wait. Don't you need a ride home?"

Ethan gave him a pointed look. "This is not a conversation I want to stick around for, son. I'll head over to the brew pub for a beer. You can join me there, if you want."

His father lifted a hand in greeting to Kate as he walked past her vehicle toward the downtown. She opened her door and climbed out and then it was just the two of them in the sun-drenched parking lot. Overhead, gulls swooped and screamed and a distant clanging of bells announced the raising of the harbor bridge to allow a sailboat to pass below.

"Hey," he said, trying to read her expression, but her dark sunglasses hid her eyes.

"Is this the new boat?" She stood by the driver's open door and her voice sounded stiff and polite.

"Yes."

"I came by the other morning, but you'd already gone out to sea." She visibly swallowed. "We need to talk."

Even if he hadn't heard the tightness in her voice, Holden would have known she was upset. In his whole life, he'd never known a conversation to go well when it began with those four words. He took a cautious step toward her, determinedly tamping down his rising unease.

"What is it? What's wrong?"

She clutched the top of the open door with one hand until the knuckles were white. Her face looked pale and pinched and her mouth was a flat line. As he approached, she closed the door and pulled her sunglasses off and Holden felt a frisson of true alarm. Her gray eyes, usually so soft and gentle, seemed uncharacteristically flat. She was studying him carefully, her gaze moving over his features as if she was seeing them for the first time. Before he realized her intent, she stepped forward and traced a finger lightly over the crooked bridge of his nose. Only supreme effort kept him from jerking away.

"I never asked you how you broke your nose," she finally

said, her voice deceptively mild. "All these years we've known each other and yet the subject has never come up."

Holden's heart twisted. "Kate—"

She dropped her hand, but not her gaze, which had turned steely. "Tell me how you broke your nose, Holden. Tell me *who* broke it."

His mind worked furiously to find the right words, reluctant to admit what he had done all those years ago. "What does it matter?"

"It matters to me!" she cried, and her composure slipped for just a second before she swiftly reschooled her features. "It *matters*."

Holden suppressed a regretful sigh. He'd known this day might come, had hoped when it did they might laugh about it but clearly that was not going to be the case. "Just hear me out, okay? I hated that you were so unhappy when I saw you that day on campus. No matter how I might have felt, Jack had an obligation to you and the baby."

"So you—what? You flew to Texas and confronted him?"

"You're damned right I did," he retorted. "Did you think I was just going to stand by and do nothing?"

"But Jack refused to give up his football dream in order to marry me, didn't he?" she demanded, her gray eyes flashing. "He probably told you to go to hell, and the two of you got into a physical brawl. But the Jack I knew wouldn't have let anyone —not even you—force him to do something he didn't want to do. So tell me what you did to change his mind."

Holden pushed his fingers into his hair and desperately wished this confrontation was over, but he also dreaded that moment because he knew it would mean the end of whatever hope he still clung to. It would mean the end of them. "Kate," he groaned, "please don't ask me that."

"Just tell me!"

"Okay," he soothed. "Fine."

But how to tell her about the ugly altercation? He'd found Jack in his dorm room with a pretty blonde who had bolted as soon as she saw Holden's expression. When Holden had demanded to know why Jack hadn't returned Kate's calls, his former friend had grown defensive and angry. Holden understood—Jack didn't want the responsibility of being a father, but this was *Kate* they were talking about. Holden would have given her anything her heart desired. If she'd wanted the moon and the stars, he would have figured out a way for her to have them. Jack was easy by comparison.

Now Kate watched him expectantly.

"He plagiarized his college entry essay," he continued, his tone grim. "I threatened to expose him to the college admissions board if he didn't marry you." He deliberately skipped over the part where Jack had taken a swing at him, triggering a brawl that had nearly destroyed the dorm room and resulted in injuries to both of them. "I don't know what they might have done—maybe suspended him for a semester—but I told Jack he'd probably lose his football scholarship. Whether that was true or not, I don't know. I never expected he would quit school. I honestly believed the two of you would get married and live on the Texas A&M campus so he could keep playing."

Kate stared at him in growing dismay. "So you blackmailed him into marrying me?" She put a hand to her forehead and turned partially away from him as she processed his words, before spinning back to confront him. "What do you mean he plagiarized his essay? How would you even know if he did?"

"Because it was my essay, Kate," he said wearily. "I wrote an essay in that college prep class we had to take and Jack stole it. He submitted it as his own."

"No." Her voice trembled with disbelief and she shook her head in denial. "He wouldn't do that."

"He didn't even bother denying it, Kate. We both know Jack was a superlative athlete but he struggled academically. If there was an easy way out, he took it." He spread his hands in a supplicating gesture. "I'm sorry. I honestly believed I was doing the right thing for you and Ryan."

Her eyes were huge and wounded as she stared accusingly at him. "You backed him into a corner, Holden. If he'd lost his scholarship, he would have had to withdraw from school and he never would have been able to face his father. He would have been a disgrace, a failure. A *cheat*." She gave a choked sob. "At least now I know the truth—the only reason he married me is because you made him feel he didn't have any other option."

"That's not true," Holden said, his voice low and grating. "He always had options. He could have stayed in school. You and the baby could have lived with him either on or off campus."

"No, Holden, that wasn't a possibility," she said in a choked voice. "We would have had no money or income to survive. Between football and school, Jack wouldn't have been able to work and I couldn't support us, not with a baby. His only option was to leave school. *You* made that happen."

"But he married you," Holden argued. "Isn't that what you wanted?"

"Not like that." She swiped furiously at her eyes. "I never wanted him to feel forced into it." She gave a bitter laugh. "At least now it all makes sense...his restlessness, his unhappiness. We tried to make a go of it, but marriage to me was never what he wanted. Not really. He began to resent me for everything he'd been forced to give up."

Holden had a hard time dredging up any sympathy for Jack because he'd had everything Holden had wanted for himself. Still wanted. He'd had Kate.

"I'm sorry," he finally managed to say. "I thought I was

doing the right thing. I should have just kept my nose out of it, but I couldn't stand seeing you so miserable."

Kate looked at him as if something had just occurred to her. "What did you mean when you said Jack had an obligation to me and Ryan, no matter how you felt?"

"What?"

"A few minutes ago, you said *no matter how you might have felt,* Jack had an obligation to me." She paused. "What did you mean? How did you feel?"

"Don't you know, Kate?" he asked gently. "Haven't you ever guessed?"

She folded her arms around her middle as if protecting herself. "Guessed what?"

Holden debated with himself for less than a second before deciding he had nothing to lose. He'd hung back for too long, let himself blend into the fabric of her life as if he were no different than a piece of her furniture. Regardless of the outcome, he needed to tell her how he felt. If he didn't, he would regret it for the rest of his life.

"I've been crazy about you for as long as I can remember, since we were kids. The hardest thing I ever did was watch you marry Jack, knowing he didn't deserve you." He stared intently at her. "I was completely head over heels in love with you. You must have guessed how I felt—how I still feel."

She shook her head, her expression one of dismay and confusion. "No, not back then. Why would I?" She paused as if a thought occurred to her. "Were you were jealous of him? Your best friend?"

Holden hesitated, torn between protecting Jack's image and telling Kate the truth. But regardless of the potential consequences to himself, he found he couldn't lie to Kate. "Jack and I stopped being friends the night he asked you to dance with him at that last high school dance. Do you remember?"

She gave a jerky nod and swiped at her cheek as a single tear spilled over. Holden pushed his hands into his front pockets to prevent himself from reaching for her. He felt as if his heart were cracking open.

"He was supposed to ask you to dance with me," he continued softly. "I'd been gathering my courage all night to ask you myself when he offered to do it for me. He said I'd have a better chance of getting you to agree if he smoothed the way first." He gave her a rueful smile. "We both know how that turned out."

"I didn't know. But when you came to see me at college—you should never have gotten involved, don't you see?" Twin patches of hectic color stained her cheeks and her expression was strained and tight. "I was wrong to even tell you about the baby."

"But you did. What was I supposed to do once I knew? Stand by while he just breezed through life without any consequences for what he'd done?"

"What about the consequences to me?" She pressed a hand to her chest for emphasis. "Did it ever occur to you that by forcing him to marry me, I would be the one to suffer? I spent more time alone during our marriage than I did with him. He couldn't wait to deploy and get away from me, and I never knew what I had done wrong, or why I wasn't enough to make him want to stay home. I wasted ten years of my life trying to make him happy when all he ever wanted was to be free."

"Kate—" He reached for her, but she flinched away.

"No, don't say anything. You've already done enough." She dragged in a ragged breath and lifted her chin, blinking back tears. "I think it would be better if you just—just stay out of my life, Holden."

Then, as Holden watched in stunned disbelief, she turned and walked away from him.

CHAPTER
FOURTEEN

The sun was low in the sky when Kate stepped out of the Portland train station on Monday evening. She scanned the line of parked cars, looking for a black pickup truck, but Holden wasn't there and her already dismal spirits sank even lower. Instead, Erin stood on the opposite curb, waving her arm to capture her attention. Hitching her bag higher on her shoulder, Kate wove through the people and cars until she reached her sister.

"Hi," Erin said with a searching look. "How was your trip?"

"Fine."

True to his word, Paul had picked her up just before ten o'clock that morning and they had arrived in Harvard Square shortly after noon. His new bakery, Maison Bellecourt, occupied a prime location just off the square where college students, locals, and tourists thronged the sidewalks. The pastry shop itself had been designed in the style of a true Parisian pâtisserie, with a glossy black exterior and the name of the shop displayed in oversized, gold-gilt letters across the storefront. The interior had still been under construction, but Kate had loved the black and white tiled floor and the hand-blown chandeliers. The dark, antique display shelves and counters lent the space an authentic, Old World feel. In contrast, the kitchen had been light-filled and airy and equipped with every modern accoutrement needed for creating sumptuous pastries and desserts.

"So what did you think?" Erin asked, when they were in the car and had merged onto the northbound highway. "Did it tempt you?"

"Very much," Kate said, recalling Paul's enthusiasm as they'd toured the pastry shop. "Paul spared no expense. The kitchen is a pastry chef's dream. The shop has both indoor and outdoor customer seating, a massive coffee bar where you can get pretty much any hot beverage you can dream of, and they also plan to serve alcohol."

Erin shot her a surprised look. "Really? So he's going for a much wider clientele than just desserts and breakfast pastries."

Kate nodded. "Yes. He feels he's competing with the Italian pastry shops in the North End. He intends to keep the shop open from seven in the morning until midnight every day. He wants it to be the premiere after-dinner destination for people looking for dessert and a coffee or cocktail."

"So you were impressed, I take it."

"Overwhelmed is more like it," Kate confessed. "I had no idea he had such big plans for the pastry shop."

"And what about the condo?"

Kate recalled the moment when they had stepped off the private elevator directly into the luxury apartment, which commanded views of the Charles River and the Boston skyline. The sun-drenched living room had boasted gleaming, polished surfaces and sleek, modern furnishings that had left Kate speechless. In her wildest imaginings, she couldn't envision herself and her son living there. As upscale as it had been, there had been nothing warm or inviting about the space. Even the gourmet chef's kitchen had felt soulless and sterile to her. But she'd smiled and said all the right things because Paul had so obviously expected her to be impressed. And she had been.

"The condo was amazing, like something out of *Lifestyles of the Rich and Famous*," she said in response to her sister's querying look.

"Well, Paul Bellecourt is both, so I guess that was to be expected," Erin said wryly. "Will you take the job? And the condo?"

"I don't know. I'm not sure I could be happy there," Kate admitted. "I had pictured a quaint little bakery, not this crazy busy night spot."

"When do you need to decide?"

"Soon." Paul had asked her to make a decision within the next few weeks so as not to miss the start of the culinary school he wanted her to attend. "There's just so much to think about."

"Did he mention a salary?"

"Yes." Kate pulled a face. "It's more than I could ever to hope to make if I stayed in Bittersweet Harbor, but I'm trying to at least pretend to be objective about my decision."

"And...did he make a pass at you?"

Kate threw her sister a startled look. "How did you—" She broke off as she realized what she had almost revealed. "What makes you think he would?"

"He did!" Erin cried. "I knew it. Of course, he'd be an idiot not to. Look at you—beautiful, smart...of course he hit on you."

"Oh, Erin, it was so embarrassing!" Kate said, putting her hands over her face. A self-conscious laugh escaped her as she recalled the awkward moment when Paul had tried to kiss her in the apartment. "I honestly had no idea, he never let on until suddenly he was right there, trying to kiss me."

"What did you do?"

Lowering her hands, Kate gave her sister a wry grin.

"Nothing I want to tell you. Suffice it to say, the whole thing was mortifying for both of us."

Reaching over, Erin squeezed her hand. "I'm sorry. Will it impact your decision?"

Kate had already come to a decision about the job even before Paul had made his pass at her. No matter how much money he offered her, she didn't think she could work for him. After his failed attempt to kiss her, she'd had an unhappy suspicion that in the end, the price she'd pay would be too high. She hated to admit that Holden had been right about everything. But Kate was also pragmatic enough to realize her emotions were running high right now and she might not be thinking clearly. Despite her misgivings, she owed it to herself to think about Paul's offer from a practical standpoint.

"It's an incredible opportunity," she finally said. "I'm going to sleep on it. I won't decide anything until I've had time to think about it and talk to Ryan."

"Good idea." Erin cast her a cautious look. "Is everything else okay? How are things with Holden?"

Kate's chest hitched at the mention of his name. She hadn't been able to stop seeing Holden's expression when she'd told him to stay out of her life. He'd looked stricken, as if he'd experienced a physical blow. In the two days since their confrontation, she'd thought of nothing else. She'd had trouble sleeping and her eyes felt dry and gritty, and there seemed to be a permanent lump in the back of her throat. She felt seconds away from bursting into tears just thinking about Holden and had spent hours berating herself for how she'd reacted.

"Things are...over between us," she said quietly.

"Oh." Erin was silent for a moment. "Can I ask what happened? The last time we talked, everything seemed to be going so well."

Kate twisted her hands together on her lap and nodded,

fixing her gaze out the car window. "They were. But I found out some stuff that makes it hard for me to forgive him."

"Wow. I can't even imagine what that might be. He seems like such a great guy and he obviously cares about you and Ryan." Erin paused. "Can you tell me what he did?"

Kate hitched a shoulder in a half-shrug. "It was a long time ago. You'll probably say it doesn't even matter."

"Well it obviously does if you've ended things with him." Erin was quiet for a moment. "Does it have anything to do with Jack?"

Kate turned to look at her sister, trying to decide how much to share. More than anything, she didn't want pity. She hated admitting that her marriage had not been great, especially in light of the sacrifices she and Jack had both made. Now, knowing the true extent of what Jack had given up, she felt ashamed because on some level she had known he didn't want to marry her, but she hadn't cared. She'd naively envisioned herself creating a cozy, blissful home for their little family, firm in the belief that he would eventually come around and be happy in his new role of husband and father—that he would value her and the effort she made to make him comfortable. That he would even be grateful.

"If I tell you, you have to promise not to repeat it to anyone," she cautioned. "Everyone in this town still remembers and adores Jack and I wouldn't want that to change."

"Okay," Erin agreed. "You know you can tell me anything."

By time Kate had haltingly related everything, they had reached the exit for Bittersweet Harbor. "So that's it," Kate said, feeling hollowed out. "And then I told him to stay out of my life."

"You were angry and everything you thought you knew about Jack had just been turned upside down," Erin said soothingly. "Your reaction was normal, but I think you're looking at it the wrong way."

Kate gave an inelegant snort. "What other way is there to look at it? Jack felt forced into marrying me and our marriage was a sham and it was all because of Holden. Worse, he pretended to be our friend."

She didn't miss the exasperated look Erin gave her. "Pretended? Really? I know you don't believe that."

Kate had the grace to flush. Recalling all the times Holden had come by to check on her and Ryan while Jack had been deployed, she knew she was being unfair. It was only now, in hindsight, that she realized Holden had never come by to visit when Jack had been home. "He still had no right to interfere the way he did."

"Maybe not, but look at it from his view—he saw the girl he loved being treated badly. He could have done any number of things. He could have taken advantage of the situation and tried to worm his way into your life. He could have told you right then that Jack wasn't worthy of you—and why. But he didn't and you know why?"

Kate cast her a cautious look. "Why?"

"Because your happiness meant more to him than his own. You wanted to marry Jack and no matter how Holden felt about that, he wanted you to be happy. So even though it went against everything *he* wanted, he made sure you got what *you* wanted." Erin made tsking sound. "He's not the villain in this story, sis."

Holden's words came back to Kate.

I've been crazy about you for as long as I can remember, since we were kids.

Was Erin right? Had Holden really felt that way about her all those years ago? And if he had, how had she never guessed? She'd been so hurt and angry when she'd thought about everything she and Jack had given up, but had Holden also made sacrifices? Had he willingly let her go despite his own feelings, because he had believed she wanted Jack?

"Here we are," Erin said, pulling Kate from her troubled thoughts.

They were parked in front of her townhouse and the lights were on inside although it was only just beginning to get dark. "Thanks for picking me up," Kate said, reaching across the seat to hug Erin. "I'll see you tomorrow. And thanks, too, for giving me a new perspective on—on what happened."

"Call Holden," Erin urged. "He meant well and that has to count for something, right? The poor guy is probably miserable."

Just the thought of talking to Holden unleashed a torrent of anxiety in Kate's stomach. She did need to talk to him, but she had no idea what she would say. She felt unhinged and lost without his steady presence and yet she had no idea how to make things right again.

"I'll think about it." She glanced at the townhouse. "I should go in. Ryan's probably wondering what's taking me so long."

Inside, she found Ryan sitting at the kitchen island playing with his handheld gaming console. Kate set her pocketbook down and pressed a kiss against his hair. "Hi, kiddo. How was the family cookout?"

"Good," he said, not looking up. "Grandma sent some food home for you."

Kate lifted the lid of a large plastic container and saw a generous helping of barbeque chicken, potato salad and a slice of key lime pie, her father's favorite. "I'm sorry I missed it," she said. "Did you have a good time?"

He shrugged. "It was fine. Jed was there so that was pretty

cool. Also, that came for you." He nodded his chin in the direction of the kitchen table.

Turning, Kate saw a bouquet of flowers in the middle of the table and her heart gave a traitorous thump. "When did those arrive?"

"They were on the front steps when I got home."

Removing the card, she opened the small envelope. Holden's signature was scrawled boldly across the white card. Nothing else, just his name. Kate's first reaction was disappointment that he hadn't included a message, but as she inspected the flowers she realized he had. The bouquet was comprised entirely of deep blue hyacinth and white tulips, interspersed with delicate greenery.

Blue hyacinth for regret, white tulips for apology.

She trailed her fingertips over the blooms and tried to imagine him ordering the bouquet. Maybe he hadn't known the meaning behind the flowers in the first bunch he had sent her, but he'd definitely known what he was doing when he'd asked the florist to prepare this bouquet. She didn't know if she was ready to forgive him, but if the recent, uncomfortable weight that had settled into her chest was any indication, she probably should. She missed him.

"By the way," Ryan said, glancing up from his video game, "we don't have school on Wednesday and Holden asked if I wanted to take his new boat out that day. I told him I did."

Kate frowned and turned away from the flowers to look at her son. "Why don't you have school?"

"Teachers' workshop."

"Well, I'm sure there are plenty of other things you could do instead of spending the day on Holden's boat. In fact, don't you have a science project that's due next week?"

"It's like ninety-nine percent finished and, anyway, it's at school. I can't bring it home to work on." He shot his mother a dark look. "I know you guys had some kind of fight, but that has nothing to do with me. Holden and I are still friends and I want to go out on his new boat."

"What makes you think we had a fight?"

"Mom." He looked exasperated. "Everyone knows! You weren't the only ones at the marina that day."

Kate stared at him in dismay even as she tried frantically to recall exactly what had been said and who might have overheard. Inwardly, she rebuked herself for having confronted Holden so publicly about something that should have been private. She had only herself to blame—she'd been so upset when she'd learned the extent of his involvement that she hadn't been thinking straight.

Now his words replayed over and over again in her head: *I was completely head over heels in love with you. You must have guessed how I felt—how I still feel.*

She recalled all the times over the course of the past fifteen years when he had come over to check on her and Ryan, how he had always taken care of them. How he still did. She'd come to rely on him, on his solid, reassuring presence in her life. Whenever a problem presented itself, he made sure she never faced it alone. The thought of him not being there caused her heart to clench painfully in her chest. She'd pushed him away when all she really wanted was to keep him close, because she'd fallen desperately and completely in love with him.

She didn't know exactly when that had happened—maybe the night they'd gone to dinner. Maybe earlier, when he'd picked her up at the train station. Maybe years ago, when he seemed to always be at her apartment performing small services for her. All she knew was that at some point along the way, she had fallen in love with Holden, but she'd been too blind to realize it. Meanwhile, he'd been showing her how much he loved her with his actions. For years, he'd been telling her he loved her, but she hadn't understood until now.

She had fallen in love with Holden.

Even the knowledge that he'd practically forced Jack to marry her didn't alter the fact that she was crazy about him, which in itself was worrying. She should be furious. She *was* furious! There was no telling how her life might have turned out or what she might have accomplished if he hadn't interfered. But another voice whispered he could be hers now, if she'd only forgive him. She could still have a happily-ever-after.

"So can I go?"

Kate forced herself to pull her scattered thoughts together and focus on her son. "What?"

"Can I go out on the boat with Holden on Wednesday?"

"Oh, I'm not sure it's a great idea—"

Ryan pushed abruptly to his feet. "So...what? I'm supposed to just pretend he doesn't exist because you're mad at him?"

"It's complicated, sweetheart. And I'm not mad at him, exactly. I just learned about some stuff he did a long time ago, and it caught me off-guard."

"So if it was so long ago, you should just let it go," Ryan said, his face hopeful. "Why does it matter anymore?"

"You don't know anything about it," Kate said stiffly, refusing to tell Ryan the nature of the argument. He was too young to understand and she would never do or say anything that might cast his father in a bad light. He had hero-worshipped his dad. "What Holden did—"

"Forget it," Ryan said. "I'll just tell Holden that you're too stubborn to let bygones be bygones. That's if I even see him again because you'll probably say I shouldn't talk to him, either."

Kate sighed and threw up her hands. "Fine. Go ahead and

go with him on Wednesday. I'll even pack you a cooler. Happy now?"

"*Yes.*" Ryan grinned. "Thanks, Mom. You're the best. I'll let him know."

As he bolted up the stairs to his bedroom, Kate thought maybe her son was right. She should just let the past go and concentrate instead on her future—one that hopefully included Holden Foster.

CHAPTER

FIFTEEN

The diner was busy the following day, but Kate had made a decision. She planned to drive to Holden's house that afternoon and tell him how she felt, even though the prospect terrified her. What if he'd changed his mind? What if their altercation at the marina had made him decide she wasn't worth fighting for? She didn't know any man who enjoyed drama and Holden struck her as a guy who would avoid it at any cost. As she piled plates onto a tray and prepared to carry them into the dining area, her phone buzzed loudly in her apron pocket. Erin glanced at her from where she was cooking at the industrial-sized griddle.

"Your phone has been going crazy today," she observed. "What's going on?"

"My mother-in-law. She's been trying to reach me for the last hour."

"Well, call her back," Erin advised. "Hopefully it's nothing serious."

Helen and Brian had always seemed bigger than life to Kate. Helen had been a cornerstone of Bittersweet Harbor society in her younger days. Now retired, Brian had been the fire chief when Kate and Jack had first married and he knew everyone in town. As a new bride and young mother, Kate had been intimidated by both of them, believing they didn't think she was good enough for their only son. Over the ensuing years of her marriage, she'd found Helen to be a kind and loving woman but she had never fully won over Brian. He'd remained aloof and critical and even Ryan wasn't spared from his caustic manner. She dreaded calling them back, but a lull in customers gave her the opportunity to step outside and dial Helen's number.

"Hello, dear," the older woman answered the phone. "I hope I haven't interrupted you at work."

"No, things have finally slowed down a bit. Is everything okay?"

"Oh, yes, but Brian and I would like you to come by the house when you've finished working. We have something we need to talk to you about."

Kate's stomach immediately knotted with anxiety. She had any number of ideas about what they might want to discuss, including her relationship with Holden, the job offer from Paul Bellecourt, or maybe Ryan's future.

"Can you tell me what it's about?" she ventured.

"It would be better face to face," came the cryptic response, which only deepened Kate's unease.

"Okay, then. I should be there around four o'clock, if that works."

"Wonderful. We'll see you then."

The rest of Kate's shift passed in a blur as she tried to guess what they needed to speak to her about. When finally, she and Erin locked the door to the diner, she drew in a deep breath.

"Maybe I should go home first and freshen up."

Erin gave her an encouraging look. "You look fine. Better to just go and get it over with."

Kate nodded. "You're right."

As they walked across the parking lot toward Kate's car, Erin glanced at her. "Have you called Holden yet?"

"No. He sent flowers yesterday, as an apology. I'm going to stop by his house after I see Helen and Brian."

"So you've decided to forgive him?"

They paused beside Kate's car and Erin waited as she fumbled in her handbag for her keys. "I've had some time to think about what happened."

"And—?"

"It was so long ago and he meant well." She gave her sister a watery smile. "I'm not sure there are many guys who would have done what he did."

"It couldn't have been easy watching you marry his best friend," Erin said, her voice gentle.

"He said it was the hardest thing he ever did and that Jack didn't deserve me."

"I'm not saying another word," Erin replied, but her expression said she agreed with Holden's view. "Call me later and let me know how it went."

"I will," Kate promised.

Once in the car, she called Ryan to let him know she would be late getting home.

"Do you want me to come with you?" he asked, and Kate's heart swelled because he so obviously wanted to support her.

"No, of course not," she assured him. "I'll be home as soon as I can. If you're hungry, there's leftover chicken in the fridge, or you can go ahead and order a pizza."

"That's okay, I'll wait for you."

Her nerves were more than a little on edge when she pulled into the driveway of the large house where Jack had grown up. Her overactive imagination had her convinced Helen and Brian had learned about her relationship with Holden and wanted to communicate their disapproval. She also wondered if they had discovered Paul Bellecourt had offered her a job in Cambridge and now wanted to tell her all the reasons why she couldn't leave town, taking their only grandson with her. But Helen's face was wreathed in smiles when she answered the door and she greeted Kate with a warm hug and kiss on the cheek.

"Hello, dear," she said, ushering her deeper into the house. "Thank you for coming by, especially when I know how tired you must be after working all day. Brian and I have some news we'd like to share with you. Please, come sit down. Would you like something to drink, maybe a cup of coffee?"

"That would be nice, thank you," Kate replied.

While Helen went into the kitchen, Brian rose from his chair and gave her a perfunctory kiss on the cheek. "Nice to see you, Kate."

"You, too," she murmured, and took a seat on the sofa as Helen returned with a tray of coffee and a plate of gingersnap cookies.

"Here you are," she said, setting the tray down on the coffee table and handing a cup to Kate.

That was when Kate saw the thick folder that lay beside the tray, with the name of a local law firm in gold letters across the front. Her heart gave an alarmed lurch. Why would they have consulted with a lawyer? She lifted her coffee cup, trying to keep the delicate china from clattering against the saucer. As she took a cautious sip, Brian picked up the folder.

"Helen and I have sold the house and we're relocating to South Carolina."

Later, Kate would be proud of herself for not dropping her cup or choking on her mouthful of coffee. Instead, she carefully placed her cup back on the coffee table and looked to Helen for confirmation, because surely she must have misheard.

"It's true," Helen said with a smile. "It's something we've

been talking about for a few years and now that Brian is retired —well, it just seems like a good time."

"But you've lived here your entire lives," Kate protested.

"That's true. But we're not getting any younger and there's so much we'd still like to do."

"But can't you do that here, in Bittersweet Harbor?"

"The only thing keeping us here is you and Ryan," Brian said, his voice gruff. "But he's getting to the age where he doesn't want to spend his time with a couple of old farts, and in a few years he'll head off to college."

"It's not just that," Helen added. "The winters don't get any easier as you get older and we both want to be somewhere warm. Now that Brian is retired, the time seems right."

Kate looked between the two of them. "So it's a done deal? The house is really sold? But I never even saw a sale sign!"

"An offer was made—a very generous offer—before the house even had a chance to be listed. We close in just a few weeks," Brian confirmed, indicating the folder in his hands. "We've already purchased a new home in South Carolina."

"A condo, really," Helen clarified. "It's in a senior community with lots of amenities and activities and we're really looking forward to the change."

"When will you move?" Kate asked, stunned by the announcement.

"If everything goes to plan, we should be in our new home by the Fourth of July," Helen said. "We hope you and Ryan will come and visit often."

"Of course," Kate said, reaching out to clasp the older woman's hand. "I'm just having a hard time processing everything."

"There's more," Brian said, his voice brusque. "We know you've been offered a job by that television pastry chef."

Here it was. The other shoe was about to drop and Kate inwardly braced herself for whatever came next. "Yes."

"In Cambridge?" Helen asked, her eyes gently inquisitive.

"That's right, but nothing's been decided yet," Kate said stiffly. "I have a lot to think about and I want to be sure whatever decision I make is the best one for both Ryan and me."

"I'm glad to hear it," Brian replied, and for the first time, Kate saw something like approval in his blue eyes. "And I hope we can make that decision a little bit easier for you."

Kate frowned. "I'm not sure I understand."

Helen beamed as she squeezed Kate's fingers. "We've lived in this house for nearly forty years. Meanwhile, the town has been growing and becoming something of a summer destination. People want to live here, but our real estate agent said there's a shortage of homes for sale in the area." She and Brian exchanged a look. "The buyers paid more than the asking price to prevent us from listing it. Much more, actually. We never expected to get the amount we did and we'd like to share our good fortune with you."

Kate's heart had begun to thump hard in her chest. "You don't need to do anything."

"You were married to our son," Brian said. "You're like a daughter to us and we want you and Ryan to be comfortable."

"We're gifting you two-hundred thousand dollars," Helen said with a smile. "You can use it however you'd like, but I'm rather hoping you'll open your own pastry shop here in Bittersweet Harbor."

Kate gasped. For a moment she couldn't even speak and her head swam. "But...how? Why? Surely you can't afford to do this!"

"Brian still has his pension, we've managed to save a fair amount over the years and as I said, the house sold for a very good price," Helen replied. "Not only can we afford to do this, we want to."

"I've also sold the Barracuda," Brian added. "Didn't seem right to let it sit in the garage any longer. The money will more than pay for Ryan's college tuition, if he goes to a state school."

"You sold the muscle car?" Kate spluttered. She knew how much the car meant to her father-in-law. It had been the final project he had worked on with Jack.

"Jack would have wanted the money to go to his son," Brian said. "Helen and I know you've been saving for Ryan's college, but we don't want you to struggle. We know your dream has been to open your own bakery and we hope our gift will allow you to do that."

"I'm sure you don't want to leave Bittersweet Harbor," Helen said, before adding gently, "Or Holden Foster."

Kate turned stricken eyes to the older woman. "We've never —he never—"

"He's a good man," Helen said. "We've known him since he and Jack were boys and I can't think of anyone I'd rather see you with."

"Jack was a good man, too," Brian said, his voice gruff with emotion. "But he had his demons. We know life wasn't always easy for you or Ryan, and we just want you to be happy. If Holden is who you want, you have our blessing."

Kate hadn't been aware she'd started to cry until Helen gave a sympathetic cluck and gathered her in for a hug. "I'm so sorry," she gulped. "I'm just so overwhelmed and grateful."

Helen laughed softly. "I understand. It's a lot to take in."

"I'll have the bank deposit the money directly into your account," Brian said. "It's a gift, so you won't be required to pay any taxes."

"Thank you," Kate finally managed, pulling away from

Helen and accepting a napkin to dry her face. "I don't know what else to say except thank you so much."

"Following your dream and opening a bakery will be thanks enough," Brian said.

An hour later, when she arrived home to share her good news with Ryan, she decided they should celebrate with dinner at his favorite restaurant. She would wait until the following day to tell Holden about her unexpected windfall and her decision to stay in Bittersweet Harbor—with him, if he would have her.

CHAPTER
SIXTEEN

K ate pulled into the marina early the following morning to drop Ryan off. She'd packed a large cooler and had added some of Holden's favorites, including her decadent chocolate bourbon cupcakes with butter pecan frosting. As they climbed out of the car, she paused to admire Holden's new boat, tied up to alongside the wharf. She had called him the previous night when she and Ryan had returned home from dinner but he hadn't answered. She hoped it was because he hadn't seen the call come in and not because he'd deliberately chosen to ignore it. Aside from her son, he'd been the first person she'd wanted to share her good news with. She wanted to share everything with him and when he hadn't picked up, some of the excitement of the day had waned. She hoped to tell him about the gift this morning.

"It's so much bigger than the Emily Ann," she observed now, looking at the boat. "Are you sure it's not too big for you and Holden to manage?"

"There's three of us. We'll be fine," Ryan assured her. "Bigger just means we can drop and haul more traps, but everything else is the same—only newer."

"Okay, well I want to talk to Holden before you head out, so I'll help you carry the cooler down to the boat."

"I can carry it," he said, and hefted it in his arms before she could argue.

She followed him down the gangway to the wharf, but when they reached the boat it became clear Holden wasn't on board. Instead, a young man whom Kate didn't recognize stepped out of the cabin.

"You must be Ryan," he said, reaching over the side of the boat to take the cooler from him. "I'm Corey Sullivan, the new sternman. Good to meet you."

"Where is Holden?" Kate asked.

"He ran over to the marine store to pick something up," Corey said. "Should be back soon if you want to wait."

Kate glanced at her watch, torn with indecision. "I wish I could, but I really need to get to work." She turned to Ryan. "You'll be okay?"

He rolled his eyes. "I'll be fine, Mom."

"Of course you will be. Have fun. And remember, it's our secret until I can tell Holden about the money myself, okay?"

Ryan zipped his fingers across his mouth. "Got it. I won't tell him anything."

Kate hesitated, still undecided about whether to wait for Holden or head over to the diner before she was late for her shift. Seeing her indecision, Ryan grasped her by the shoulders and turned her in the direction of the parking lot. "Go, or Auntie Erin will have a fit. I'll text you when we're underway, okay?"

"Okay," she said, laughing in spite of herself. "I'll be here at four o'clock to pick you up. Will you tell Holden that I need to speak to him when you get back?"

"Sure, Mom."

At the top of the gangway she paused and looked back at

the boat. Corey was dumping more bait into the bait cooler and Ryan was pulling on a pair of rubber overalls. Seeing her watching, he lifted a hand and then gave her an expectant look, as if asking her why she was still there. Disappointed that she hadn't had an opportunity to talk with Holden, she returned to her van and drove the short distance to the other side of the harbor. The diner was already half full when she arrived, so she quickly filled the glass pastry display with a selection of her muffins, cupcakes and pastries, before ducking into the kitchen.

"Good morning," Erin called from where she was cooking eggs and hash browns on the grill. "I half expected you to take the day off today after yesterday's bombshell."

When Kate hadn't been able to reach Holden the previous night, she'd called Erin and they had talked for nearly an hour. After her initial stunned disbelief, Erin had promised to help Kate locate an affordable storefront for her pastry shop.

"I would never leave the diner in the lurch," Kate said, smiling. "But I do think we need to consider bringing on one or two extra wait staff. If everything works out the way I hope, I won't be able to continue working here every day."

"Or any day," Erin said. "Running your own business is a full-time job." She pulled a face. "I should know."

Although the All Shook Up Diner was a family-owned business, Erin was the driving force behind the restaurant's success. In addition to being the head cook, she also managed the ordering of food and supplies, oversaw the finances and administered the payroll. Without Erin, there would be no diner.

"You work too hard," Kate said, double-checking the plates of food as Erin slid them under the warmer. "Maybe we should consider bringing another cook on board, too."

Erin cut her a quelling look. "Never. I'm just conceited enough to believe nobody can cook as well as I can."

"You may be right," Kate laughed as she gathered the plates and pushed through the swinging doors that led from the kitchen to the diner. In a booth by the windows sat four older women, all members of the Bittersweet Harbor council on aging. They came for breakfast at the diner every Wednesday morning and Kate enjoyed chatting with them.

"Good morning, Kate," chirped Mrs. Benson, the council's president. "You appear very cheerful this morning and I think we can all guess why." She shared a knowing glance with the other women in the booth and they all tittered.

"Oh, and what reason would that be?" Kate asked with a smile as she slid the plates onto the table.

"A little birdie told me you might soon be the newest protégé of a very well-known pastry chef."

A known blabbermouth, Mrs. Benson delighted in sharing rumors and gossip, but Kate ruefully acknowledged she was also well-connected in town and generally knew anything of interest that might be happening.

"Ah, that. I'm sorry to say you've been misinformed, Mrs. Benson. You see, I'm actually looking to open my own pastry shop right here in town." Reaching for the coffee pot, Kate refilled each of their mugs. "If you happen to know of a store-front for rent, maybe you could let me know?"

She grinned as Mrs. Benson's eyes rounded in surprise and felt just a little gleeful that, for once, Mrs. Benson didn't know *everything* that happened.

"Well, we shall certainly keep our ears to the ground," Mrs. Benson declared. "Won't we, ladies? And while you're here, I'll take one of your blueberry coffeecake muffins."

"Of course, Mrs. Benson."

The morning passed quickly and they were halfway through the lunch rush when Savannah burst through the door, her face pale and tight with anxiety. Kate looked up from where she was pouring coffee at the counter and froze at the sight of her sister's face.

"What is it?" she asked, coming out from behind the counter. "What's wrong?"

Glancing at the customers, Savannah pushed Kate ahead of her through the swinging doors and into the kitchen. Erin glanced up and then did a double-take when she saw who it was.

"Hey, Savannah, what brings you here?" she asked.

Since becoming engaged to Jed Lawson, Savannah had drastically cut back her hours at the diner in order to pursue her own photography business. By all accounts, things were going well and she had a full calendar of family portrait, engagement and wedding shoots. Now she pulled Kate deeper into the kitchen and gripped her by the arms as she looked intently at her.

"You need to be strong, Kate. Jed just called me," she said. "They received a distress call and they're on their way to rescue a capsized lobster boat. It's Holden's boat."

Kate's head swam and her knees might have buckled if Savannah hadn't been holding her so firmly. "No, no, it can't be," she said, grabbing her sister's arms. "Ryan is on board with him!"

"Oh, hell." Erin grabbed Mary, one of the waitresses, and directed her to the grill. "Just keep stuff from burning," she said, before she put her arms around Kate. "It'll be okay. Holden is an experienced fisherman. He knows what he's doing and he'll keep Ryan safe."

Kate nodded as she struggled to breathe, but all she could picture was her son in the frigid waters of the Atlantic. Was he hurt? Was he drowning?

"Kate, look at me." Savannah gave her a hard shake. "He'll be okay. They'll both be okay. Remember when I fell overboard that night? I was in the water for nearly thirty minutes and I survived. Ryan and Holden will survive, too."

Savannah had fallen from a commercial party boat on the night of her high school graduation nearly seven years earlier. Fortunately, Jed Lawson had also been on board and had jumped in after her. He'd located her in the dark waters and had pulled her to the safety of a rocky island, where they'd been found by a search party hours later.

"But the water is freezing," Kate said, her own teeth beginning to chatter. "How long can they last? How long will it take the coast guard to reach them?"

"Jed said Holden is nearly forty miles offshore, but the coast guard sent a chopper and two rescue boats. They'll be there soon. We don't know what happened—the boat may still be afloat."

Kate knew what capsized meant, knew a lobster boat was as susceptible to sinking as any other vessel. The town had experienced its share of boating accidents over the years and Kate wasn't so naïve as to believe the situation wasn't very dangerous. The water temperature that far offshore was only about forty-five degrees. How long could a person survive in those conditions? Her chest felt so tight she could hardly breathe and there was a loud buzzing in her head. Her son—*her baby*—was out there in the Atlantic somewhere and she was powerless to help him. She didn't know if she could go on if anything happened to him. She tried to take some comfort in knowing Holden was with him. She knew instinctively he would do everything in his power to protect and save Ryan. But who would protect Holden?

"Here, sit down," Erin said, pulling a stepstool out of the utility closet and pushing it close. "Take some deep breaths."

"I tried to call him—Holden—last night," Kate said mournfully, sinking onto the stool. "He didn't answer and he wasn't at the marina when I dropped Ryan off. Our last words weren't good ones." With a choked sob, she leaned forward and buried her face in her hands. "What if he dies thinking I hate him? What if I lose them both?"

Savannah crouched in front of her and took Kate's hands in her own, rubbing them briskly. "They're not going to die. Jed will find them both and bring them home." She glanced over her shoulder to where Mary and Erin stood watching with solemn, worried expressions. "I'll walk with her to the house. Jed will call me as soon as he has an update."

Erin nodded. "Good idea. I'll call Mom and the others and let them know what's happened. I'll call Brian and Helen, too."

Kate nodded and stood. "Thank you. I'm sorry to run out on you like this, but—"

"Hush," Erin said. "I'm going to hang the *Closed* sign on the door and as soon as I can get away, I'll join you. Now go."

Outside, the sky was a cloudless blue and the water sparkled where it lapped against the shoreline. How was it possible that anything bad could happen on a day such as this? Was this the price she had to pay for finally having happiness within her grasp? Surely God wouldn't be so cruel as to put all her dreams within reach, only to snatch them away? Kate felt surreal as she and Savannah walked along the crushed shell roadway that led from the diner to the Belshaw family house located at the far end of Scanty Island. The sun blinded her. She closed her eyes and her son's face swam into view, lifeless and pale beneath a watery surface.

"I think I'm going to be sick," she muttered before she lurched to the side of the path and retched into the sea grass that grew there. She didn't remember walking the rest of the way to the house. She sank into an Adirondack chair on the covered porch and Savannah pushed a glass of chilled lemonade into her hand.

"Drink," she ordered.

Kate obeyed, hardly able to swallow past the constricting lump in her throat. She gazed past the Nanick Lighthouse, which stood sentry at the mouth of the wide river, to the ocean beyond. From where she sat, she could even see the Coast Guard station on the opposite shore.

"We'll be able to see the Coast Guard boats when they return, won't we?" she asked.

"We will," Savannah confirmed. "But Jed will call me before then."

Setting her glass aside, Kate pushed to her feet. "I can't stand this! I feel so useless. There must be something we can do!"

The sound of a car engine interrupted their thoughts and they turned to see Pauline Belshaw pull up beside the house. Beside her in the passenger seat was Maggie.

"We came as soon as we heard," Pauline said, climbing the steps to the porch. "Come here, darling."

Kate moved into her mother's open arms and burst into tears. "I don't know what to do. Tell me what to do!"

Savannah's phone buzzed and they pulled apart to watch as she answered. "Jed? Did you find them? Oh, thank God!" She paused and her face puckered with concern. "Oh, no. Okay, we're heading there now." She turned to Kate. "They found them. Ryan is okay."

Kate gasped and doubled over in relief, her limbs suddenly weak. "Oh, thank you, thank you," she breathed, before straightening. "And Holden?"

"Jed said he's in bad shape, Kate. They're airlifting all three of them to Portland."

"What does that mean?" Kate asked, her heart clenching.

She crossed her arms over her stomach. "What does *bad shape* mean?"

But Savannah only shook her head. "I don't know, that's all he said. He had to jump off the call before I could ask, I'm sorry."

"Okay, I'll drive," Maggie said, indicating the car. "Do Holden's parents know? Can someone call them? And what about the third guy?"

"His name is Corey Sullivan," Kate said, still trying to wrap her head around the news. "I don't know his family."

"Jed will make sure their families are contacted," Savannah assured her. "Let's focus on Ryan, who is okay. We can't know Holden's condition until we get to the hospital so there's no point in letting your imagination get the best of you."

"He's young and he's strong," Maggie said, drawing Kate toward the car. "That has to work in his favor."

The ride to the hospital seemed interminable, but knowing her son was safe eased some of Kate's worry. She clung to the fact that Holden was alive. As Maggie had said, he was physically strong. He was an experienced fisherman and he would have known what to do to survive. But her mind took her to dark places during the drive as she envisioned him trapped in the sunken vessel and unconscious in the frigid waters. What had happened to cause the boat to capsize? How long had they been in the water?

"We're here," her mother said, interrupting her troubled thoughts.

They were pulling up to the front entrance of the hospital and Kate had her seatbelt unfastened before the car had fully come to a stop.

"Wait," her mother said, and put a restraining hand on Kate's arm. "Just wait for me to come with you."

"I'll park the car and meet you inside," Maggie said when they had climbed out.

Inside, they made their way to the information center and were told all three patients had arrived by helicopter and were currently being treated in the emergency room on the first floor. When they arrived in the crowded waiting area, Kate was the first to see Holden's parents, Ethan and Laura, talking with a nurse at the check-in window. Their faces were drawn with anxiety and Kate hesitated, wondering if she should approach them. She had waited on them at the diner many times over the years, but she didn't know them well. Then Laura turned and Kate saw the anguish in her eyes. A fist closed over her heart and she had to cover her mouth with her hand to prevent a cry. There was only one reason for Holden's mother to look so agonized. As Kate watched, paralyzed, Ethan led his wife toward a vacant chair, his own face twisted with worry. It was only then that Kate saw Holden's sister sitting along the wall with her friend, Samantha. Both girls looked shell-shocked.

"There are the Fosters," her mother said, and drew Kate forward. "Laura, Ethan, how is Holden?"

The other couple turned and for a moment, Laura's face cleared. "Oh, Pauline, you're here. I'm so relieved your grandson is okay. And Kate, there you are." Reaching out, she took Kate's hands in her own. "I'm so sorry for what you must be going through."

"No more than I am for you," Kate replied. "How is Holden? We've only just arrived and no one can tell us anything."

"He was hypothermic when they pulled him out of the water," Laura replied. "They're trying to regulate his body temperature now."

"But he's alive?" Kate persisted. "He'll be okay?"

Holden's parents exchanged an anguished look before

Ethan pulled his wife into his arms, where she buried her face against his shoulder.

"He was about two minutes from heart failure when they brought him in," Ethan said, his expression solemn. "They're working to stabilize him now. I won't lie to you—it's touch and go. He's not out of the woods."

SEVENTEEN

P auline put a bracing arm around Kate's shoulders as Kate sagged against her. "Let's go find Ryan, hmm?"

"What if he doesn't make it?" Kate whispered. "I'm not sure I'm strong enough to bear that. I can't lose him."

Her mother didn't pretend to misunderstand. "Holden is young and strong and healthy and he's getting the best care possible."

Kate nodded, but her thoughts were consumed with grim images of Holden fighting for his life. Jack had been young, strong and healthy, too, but that hadn't been enough to save him.

"He's not Jack, and he wasn't on a battlefield," Pauline said, accurately reading her thoughts. "He has an excellent chance at recovery, you know that."

"I know. I do," Kate said, giving her mother a wan smile.

At the nurse's window, they were directed into the emergency room itself where they were ushered past a series of drawn curtains. As they made their way deeper into the trauma unit, Kate could hear the efforts being made to diagnose and treat the patients who lay behind those curtains. Then finally, they stopped and the nurse pulled back the drape. Ryan lay on a narrow bed, covered in heated blankets with a bandage near his hairline. Seeing Kate, he pushed himself higher on his pillows and his face crumpled.

"Mom," he cried.

"Oh, honey," she said, and gathered him into her arms where he wept brokenly against her shoulder. She held him tight, breathing in his familiar boy scent and silently thanking the universe—and Holden—for returning him to her. "Are you all right? Are you hurt?"

He shook his head and pulled away, swiping at his damp cheeks. "No, I'm okay. Sorry, I didn't think I was going to do that."

"It's okay, you can cry if it makes you feel better."

But Ryan composed himself and gave her a weak smile. "Thanks. What about Holden, have you seen him?"

"Not yet, darling," she answered, and gently combed her fingers through her son's hair, stiff with sea salt. "He's in rough shape and they're working to stabilize him."

"He saved my life." He drew in a shuddering breath. "I would have died if not for him."

"Can you tell us what happened?" Pauline prompted. She had come to sit on the other side of Ryan's bed and now she gripped his hand in her own while Savannah and Maggie stood at the foot of the bed.

Ryan shook his head. "Everything happened so fast. We were about thirty-six miles offshore and the swells were three to four feet, but nothing we haven't seen before. Holden was hauling traps, Corey was baiting the empty ones and I was measuring and banding the catch. All of a sudden, Holden began shouting and throwing life vests at us. He said we were taking on water but he couldn't tell where it was coming in."

"Was the bilge pump working?" Savannah asked.

Kate looked at her sister in mild surprise. Following her own boating accident, Savannah had sworn off ever stepping foot on a boat or even venturing into the water again. Her fiancé, Jed, had changed all that, teaching her how to swim and taking her out in his own boat until she'd eventually come to enjoy the ocean again. The fact she even knew what a bilge pump was, was testament to her newfound confidence and boating skills.

"I think the water was coming in faster than the pump could handle," Ryan replied. "By then, there was about a foot of seawater on the floor and stuff was starting to float. Corey grabbed the radio to call for help. I ran into the wheelhouse to grab my phone and that's when the whole thing went over."

Kate couldn't suppress her gasp. "The boat, you mean?"

Ryan nodded. "Yup. She just flipped upside down and I was flung around in the cabin." He touched a tentative hand to the bandage on his brow. "I must have hit my head against something, but I don't remember. Corey said I was knocked unconscious. Holden swam into the cabin and pulled me out and brought me to the surface."

"You went back for your *phone*?" Savannah exclaimed in disbelief. "*Why?*"

Ryan looked at her with a mixture of alarm and embarrassment. "Because it's new and I didn't want to lose it?"

"Okay, listen up. I never told anyone this," Savannah said, shooting a wary glance at her mother, "but the night I fell overboard, I was trying to retrieve my phone."

"What?" Pauline looked surprised. "How? I thought you said it was a rogue wave."

"Well, it was...sort of," Savannah said. "But the truth is, I had accidentally dropped my phone onto the gunwale and I thought I could climb over the railing and grab it. So I was on the wrong side of the safety rail when the wave hit. I never even saw it coming."

"Savannah!" Pauline cried, looking horrified. "You never said! Does Jed know?"

"He does," Savannah admitted. "He actually saw me on the gunwale and tried to warn me, but it was too late." She turned to Ryan. "I wasn't much older than you when it happened, which is why I'm going to tell you that your phone is never a good reason to put yourself in danger, got it?"

"Yes, Auntie," he said, looking suitably chastened.

"Did you at least have your life vest on?" Kate asked her son, striving to remain calm as the horrifying images swamped her.

"I did, but I didn't have a chance to buckle it closed and the water ripped it right off."

'Oh, my God," Kate breathed. "So the three of you made it out of the boat, and then what?"

"The boat was upside down and sinking. Holden took his own life vest off and put it on me, and then he swam back into the boat to try and grab the emergency raft, but it was too late." A weak smile curved his mouth. "Good thing you packed us a big cooler, Mom."

"Why?"

"Because after the boat went down, that cooler popped to the surface like a cork. That's what kept us afloat until help came."

"Three of you clung to that old cooler?" Kate couldn't keep the dismay out of her voice. Then, knowing what might have happened if she hadn't packed that cooler, she burst into tears.

"Mom!" Ryan exclaimed, alarmed. "Don't cry, I'm okay."

Kate wiped at her face and tried to give Ryan a reassuring smile. "I know, and I'm so grateful."

Ryan's brow puckered. "Can you find out how Holden's doing? He saved my life, Mom. And what about Corey? He was in the helicopter with me but I didn't see him after we landed."

"I'll go see what I can find out," Maggie said.

But as she turned from the curtain, she nearly collided with Brian and Helen, whose anxious faces cleared when they saw their grandson in one piece.

"Oh, thank goodness," Helen exclaimed, coming forward to clasp Ryan in a hug. "You gave us quite a scare!"

"I'm okay, Nana." He looked both pleased and a little embarrassed by all the attention, especially when Brian cuffed him gently on the shoulder and then bent to press a kiss against the top of his head.

A nurse poked her head through the curtain and seeing the six family members crowding around Ryan, gave an exclamation. "I'm sorry, but I'm going to have to limit visitors to just two people, please. If the rest of you can wait in the lounge area, you can take turns visiting, but no longer than ten minutes at a time, please."

"Mom, you and Helen should stay with Ryan," Kate said. She turned to the nurse. "I'd like to see Holden Foster, if that's possible. He was brought in with my son."

The nurse gave her an assessing look. "He's just down the hall, but I think his parents are with him."

"If I could just see him," Kate begged, her heart beginning to thump hard at the thought of seeing Holden again. "He—he saved my son's life. If I promise not to disturb him, could I just peek in at him?"

After what seemed like a long moment, the nurse relented. "Fine, but only to look." She gestured to the others who still hovered near Ryan's bed. "I'll be back in two minutes and I only want to see the grandmothers in here, got it?"

"Yes," they chorused in response and began to quietly file out of the emergency room.

"This way," the nurse said.

"Is he out of danger?" Kate asked.

"His core temperature was only eighty-six degrees when they pulled him out of the water," the nurse said. "It's slowly coming back up, but he absolutely cannot exert himself or become agitated." She glanced at Kate as if suspecting her capable of inducing uncontrollable excitement in Holden. "Doing so could cause cardiac arrhythmia."

"I understand," Kate assured her. "I just need to see for myself he's okay."

As they approached the last curtained bed, the nurse quietly pulled the fabric aside. Holden lay on the narrow bed with heating pads and blankets tucked around his body and an intravenous line inserted in one arm. He was unconscious. His parents sat on either side of the bed holding his hands. As if sensing her presence, they each turned to look at her.

"I'm sorry," Kate said as they both rose. "I don't want to disturb you, I only needed to see him."

But Laura Foster kissed her son on his forehead and then came to where Kate stood. Reaching out, she squeezed one of Kate's hands. "Of course you want to see him. Stay as long as you'd like. His father and I are going now to speak with the doctor."

As Holden's parents stepped out of the small exam area, Kate set her pocketbook down on a nearby chair and went to Holden's bedside. She drank in the sight of him, her chest constricting with the realization of how close she had come to losing him. She could still lose him, if the nurse was to be believed.

Holden's lashes were dark against his cheeks and he looked pale beneath his tan. His lips were tinged with blue and when Kate reached for his hand, there was no warmth in his fingers.

She closed her own hand carefully around his, willing her body heat and life force into him.

"How is he?"

Kate looked up to see Erin standing in the opening of the curtained room. She shook her head. "I don't know. He's alive and that's what I'm holding on to."

Erin nodded solemnly. "Okay. Ryan is desperate for news, so I'll let him know. And we'll each take turns staying with him so he won't be alone. You should stay here."

Kate nodded, her eyes welling. "Thank you."

After Erin left, Kate bent her head and prayed in a way she hadn't done since she was a child. She didn't know how long she sat at his bedside, holding his hand in her own. Hours, maybe. At times she had company—Holden's parents, his sister, various medical personnel who would take note of his vitals or readjust his blankets or replace his IV fluids. None of them asked her to leave, for which she was grateful. He'd always been there for her, now she would be there for him. At some point, she must have dozed off. A gentle pressure on her fingers brought her awake to find Holden watching her through half-closed eyes.

"*Holden.* You're awake." Relief and joy flooded through her.

"Ryan?" His voice sounded hoarse.

She wasn't surprised that his first thought was for her son.

"He's fine," she assured him, leaning forward to lay a hand against his cheek. "You saved his life, and Corey is going to be okay, too. They're both fine."

"Then why are you crying?"

Kate hadn't been aware she was until he said so. She gave him a watery smile. "Because I thought I'd lost you. Because I've been praying so hard for you to come back to me and making all kinds of crazy promises to God if only you'd be okay."

One corner of his mouth lifted in a half-smile. Kate noted his color seemed better and his lips were no longer blue. "Oh, yeah? What kinds of promises?"

She turned his hand over in hers and pressed her mouth against his palm. "To tell you how much I love you, and to never let you out of my sight again."

"That doesn't sound crazy to me," he managed, his dark eyes warm. "That sounds pretty perfect." He shrugged off the heavy, heated pad that covered his body and opened his arms. "Come here." His voice was low and rough and with a soft sob, Kate pressed herself against his chest. His arms came around her, strong and warm, and his mouth moved against her temple. "I'm here, Kate. Please, don't cry."

"I thought I'd lost you," she said again on a stifled sob, her voice muffled against his chest. "I thought I'd never have the chance to tell you how sorry I am for all the stupid things I said. I didn't mean them!"

"I know. Shh, it's okay," he said, stroking her hair. "I'm not going anywhere, I promise."

He slid one hand along her jaw and lifted her face so that she found herself only inches from his. Up close, she could see the exhaustion etched into the grooves on either side of his mouth. His eyes were bloodshot and tired, but tender as they searched hers. She wanted badly to kiss him. Even as the thought occurred to her, he bent his head and his warm mouth crushed hers. There was nothing gentle or tentative about the kiss; it was demanding and raw, almost desperate in its intensity. Kate didn't resist, she welcomed the hard pressure until finally, his lips softened and became more searching, seeking out the warmth of her mouth as if he were a drowning man and she was his last salvation. When, finally, they broke apart, their breath mingled in soft pants.

"I'm so sorry," he said softly, stroking a loose tendril of hair back from her face. "For everything I did and whatever pain I caused you, I'm sorry. Forgive me."

Kate bent her forehead to his and briefly closed her eyes. "There's nothing to forgive, Holden. Whatever unhappiness existed in my marriage had nothing to do with you. You were always my rock and my safe harbor when things got rough." She drew in an unsteady breath and searched his eyes. "Whatever's left of me is yours. If you still want me."

Holden gave a disbelieving laugh. "Want you? Honey, you're the only thing I've ever wanted. You and Ryan, both. He's really okay?"

"Yes. He's okay because you saved his life. He said you swam into the submerged cabin and pulled him out."

"Of course I did," Holden said, still caressing her jaw.

"I can never thank you enough for that."

"I don't want your gratitude," he said, his voice rough. A violent tremor shook his big frame and Kate pulled away and dragged the heated pad back over his chest.

"You're cold," she said anxiously, making sure he was completely covered. "They said your body temperature was dangerously low when they found you. Is this better? Are you feeling any warmer?"

His hands covered hers. "Kate."

She stilled and looked at him.

"I love you," he said, his eyes as dark as molasses. "I've always loved you, but I never let myself dare to believe we had any future together until recently. I know I screwed up by interfering the way I did all those years ago, but you need to know I only wanted you to be happy. When I was out there today, not knowing if we'd be rescued in time, I promised myself I would tell you how I felt the second I saw you again."

"Oh, Holden..." She was crying again, silent tears streaming down her cheeks because she knew she was being given a second chance that she likely didn't deserve. A second chance with Holden, a second chance at happiness—a second chance for everything she'd ever wanted. "I love you, too. I love you so much. Please tell me I didn't ruin it when I said those awful things to you that day."

"Ah, Kate." His mouth curved upward. "How could you, when I feel as if every dream I've ever wanted is finally coming true?"

Kate slid her hands to his face, cupping his jaw in her hands. "I love you, Holden Foster. I think I have for a while now, maybe since—" She broke off, felt herself blushing beneath his interested regard.

"Since when, sweetheart?"

"Since I started having very, uh, explicit dreams about you," she confessed. "I could barely bring myself to face you."

"Really? How long have you been having these dreams?"

"Six months, maybe more," Kate said, suddenly shy.

"My sweet girl," he murmured, and covered her mouth with his in a kiss that was both reverent and intensely sensual at the same time.

Behind them, a strident alarm began to sound and they broke apart, startled. At the same time, the curtain was pulled aside and a nurse rushed in—the same nurse who had earlier cautioned Kate about Holden's condition. When she saw Kate half-sprawled against Holden, she gave them both a withering look before she turned the alarm off on the heart monitor machine.

"I warned you about getting him excited," she said, hands on her hips. "Do I need to ask you to leave?"

"No, no," Kate said quickly. "It won't happen again."

"See that it doesn't," she said crisply, before taking Holden's vital signs. She gave a grunt but her expression held a hint of amusement when she looked at Holden. "I'm glad to see you're awake and it looks like your temperature is coming up nicely, almost back to normal. I'll just go get the doctor."

After she had left, Holden caught Kate's hand and carried it to his mouth where he pressed a warm kiss against her palm. "You lied to her."

"I did?"

"Yes," he said, pulling her back into his arms. "Because I *am* going to kiss you again, as often as possible. If I don't, I'll regret it for the rest of my life."

Kate smiled, as he turned his face and kissed her.

EPILOGUE
THREE MONTHS LATER

The Davenport Yacht Club was awash in color, with towering urns of flowers on every polished surface and swags of foamy tulle draped across the wide doorways. The long sweep of green lawn behind the historic venue had been transformed, dominated now by an enormous sailcloth tent. At least forty linen-covered tables had been set up beneath the canopy, each with a floral centerpiece and unobstructed views of the water. A fifteen-piece brass ensemble played as hundreds of couples danced beneath strings of fairy lights to the strains of a Frank Sinatra ballad. Beyond the spill of light, Kate stood with Holden at the water's edge and watched as a perfect crescent moon rose over the horizon. She leaned against his warm, solid frame, the combination of champagne and music making her feel a little heady, as if she might float away.

"Look how happy she is," she said to Holden, drawing his attention to where Savannah and Jed danced together in the center of the dance floor.

Savannah looked exquisite in a mermaid style wedding

gown, her vibrant hair spilling down her back in lustrous waves. Jed couldn't seem to take his eyes off her.

"She's happy because she didn't have to pay for this shindig," Holden said, amusement lacing his voice. "The lobster alone must have cost close to twenty grand."

Kate had to admit the wedding was over the top, but she wouldn't expect anything less from Clarissa Lawson, who by all accounts had planned and paid for everything except Savannah's gown and the wedding cake—which Kate had made, and which had drawn admiring gasps from the guests when it had been wheeled out to be cut.

"I think both Savannah and Jed would have been happy to elope, honestly," Kate replied, looping her arms around Holden's neck. He looked stunningly handsome in a classic tuxedo, the snowy whiteness of the shirt contrasting nicely with his tanned skin. His hair had been cut and tamed into obedience, although Kate decided she preferred it longer and more unruly. She caressed the newly shortened layers at his neck with her fingertips.

"Since you brought it up," Holden said, his dark eyes intent as he gazed down at her, "how would you feel about eloping?"

Kate's heart nearly stopped beating before exploding into a frenzied rhythm as she stared at him, wide-eyed. "Are you proposing?"

"I wasn't going to do this tonight, but I don't want to wait any longer to make you mine," he said. "I feel as if I've been waiting my entire life."

"But I am yours," she insisted, searching his eyes.

"I want to marry you, Kate. I want us to spend the rest of our lives together." She watched, speechless, as he went down on one knee, reached into his jacket and drew forth a small, velvet box. He snapped it open with one hand and Kate gasped when she saw the single glittering diamond set high on a gold band. It was easily two carats and seemed to catch the surrounding light and throw it back in dazzling splendor. "Kate Belshaw Prescott, would you make me the happiest man alive and be my wife?"

"Oh, Holden," she breathed. She smiled at him through tears of happiness. "Yes, yes, I'll marry you."

He stood and slid the solitaire onto her trembling finger where it sparkled and flashed. Then, uncaring of who might be watching, he kissed her.

"It's so beautiful," Kate said when they finally broke apart. She kept one hand against his broad shoulder where she could continue to admire the ring.

"Not as beautiful as you," Holden answered. "I know the bride is supposed to be the center of attention, but it's you I can't stop looking at. You're absolutely lovely."

Kate felt herself grow warm beneath his heated stare. She wore a pale blush gown that bared her shoulders, and her hair had been styled in a loose updo, with several long tendrils allowed to curl against her neck. She knew she looked good, but she would never get used to Holden's compliments, or the way he looked at her, or how he caused her pulse to race and her stomach to flutter whenever he walked into a room. The one thing she could get used to was how safe and whole and *seen* she felt when they were together.

"When should we do it?" she asked shyly.

'Soon. I hope you don't mind, but I've already spoken to Ryan about it. He said he approves."

Kate laughed. "Of course he did, he adores you."

"I couldn't be prouder of him if he were my own son," Holden said gruffly. "I thought maybe once the pastry shop is ready for the grand opening, we could escape to Aruba for a week, get married, and open the shop when we return."

After Brian and Helen had gifted her the money for the

shop, Kate had contacted Paul Bellecourt to let him know she wouldn't be accepting his offer, no matter how generous. He'd accepted her decision with good grace and had wished her luck. A month later, a small commercial building that had previously been the site of an ice-cream parlor had become available and Kate had wasted no time in securing a two-year rental agreement with the property management company. She had hired a small crew to gut the interior and install a new kitchen, as well as a service counter and display cabinets for her pastries and desserts. Holden had been invaluable, spending much of his free time helping her get the bakery ready. The grand opening of the new Bittersweet Bake Shoppe was scheduled for the first weekend in November, a scant two months away.

"What about your work?" she asked. "Can you afford to take a week off?"

"I didn't want to tell you until it was a sure thing, but the insurance settlement on the boat came in this week," Holden said. "The investigation showed the boat manufacturer was at fault for installing a livewell fitting using cheap PVC pipes. Because it was inside the livewell, it was out of sight and undetectable until it began to leak. There was also no shut-off valve and no way to stop the ingress of water once it began leaking."

"Please, stop." Kate shuddered. "Even though you all survived, I can't bear thinking about what might have happened."

"What I'm trying to tell you," Holden pressed on, "is that the insurance covered the cost of the boat and then some. I'm not going to lose any money, and I'll start looking for another boat this winter—one that I'll have carefully inspected for safety. But we can afford a very nice honeymoon."

"So we would delay the opening by a week?" Kate asked.

"Only if you agree," Holden replied. "Otherwise, we could find a justice of the peace and spend our wedding night at the

Hummingbird Inn. I don't care about the details, I just want to marry you."

"Oh," Kate murmured, "because I was thinking *two* weeks in Aruba might be nice."

Holden gave a tortured groan and pulled her into his arms. "Whatever and whenever you want, sweetheart. If you have your heart set on a big wedding, I suppose I can wait. I just want you to be happy."

"I am happy," she said, smiling, "and I don't want a big wedding. I just want you."

"Then dance with me," he murmured against her ear. "I've waited fifteen years for the perfect partner and I finally have her in my arms."

As the music swelled, he swirled her around in his arms and Kate realized he was right—they were perfect together.

The End

ALSO BY KAREN FOLEY

Bittersweet Harbor

Because of You

What's Left of Me

All-American Alphas

Anything You Want

Anything You Need

Anything at All

Love Always, Ireland

Kiss Me Under the Irish Sky

Love Me Beneath the Irish Moon

Glacier Creek

A Hummingbird Christmas

Montana Defender

Montana Firefighter

Montana Protector

Riverrun Ranch

Swipe Right for a Cowboy

Counting on the Cowboy

How to Catch a Cowboy

Firefighters of Montana

Heat

Overnight Sensation

Hot-Blooded

Heat of the Moment

Devil in Dress Blues

Hold On To the Nights

Coming Up for Air

No Going Back

God's Gift to Women

A Kiss in the Dark

Free Fall

If Only in My Dreams

Hard to Hold

Make Me Melt

ABOUT THE AUTHOR

Karen Foley is the award-winning author of 26 sexy, contemporary romances filled with confident, complex heroes and strong, smart heroines. Her books have garnered numerous accolades, including a Romantic Times Top Pick, Booksellers' Best Award, Golden Leaf Award, New England Reader's Choice finalist, RWA RITA finalist and RWA Vivian finalist. Karen believes life is better with love, chocolate, and a view of the sea. She lives in coastal New England with her high-school sweetheart, where she can be found boating, reading, or plotting her next book.

Milton Keynes UK
Ingram Content Group UK Ltd.
UKHW041001040324
438885UK00006B/386